Beneath

the Blue Mountain

Beneath
the Blue Mountain

RICHARD S. WHEELER

DOUBLEDAY & COMPANY, INC.

GARDEN CITY, NEW YORK

1979

All of the characters in this book are fictitious,
and any resemblance to actual persons, living or dead,
is purely coincidental.

ISBN: 0-385-14748-1
Library of Congress Catalog Card Number: 78-15842
Copyright © 1979 by Richard S. Wheeler
All Rights Reserved
Printed in the United States of America
First Edition

*Beneath
the Blue Mountain*

CHAPTER 1

The vaquero Jaime Ortega unsaddled the grulla and shoved him into the mesquite corrals without currying the animal. That was a violation of Don Ignacio's strict orders, but Jaime had pressing news to tell the patrón.

The bowlegged man, the color of his saddle and all whipcord, hurried across the plaza, past the casitas and the great well, and up to the long white casa of the Hacienda del Leon, the only plastered building among the tawny adobes.

The servant girl Juanita admitted him through the carved double doors and led him to the parlor, where he discovered not only Ignacio Olivera, but also el Capitán Pedro Castillo-Armas and the patrona, la Señorita Maria Louisa.

"What is it, Jaimicito?"

The vaquero clutched his grimy sombrero nervously, in the presence of so many.

"I was riding the western lands," he began uneasily. "And I found strange cattle in the rincon south of the great spike of Baboquivari. They were branded with a large H."

The capitán and Don Ignacio exchanged glances.

"Is there any more?" Ignacio asked.

"Sí. There is no water in that rincon," the vaquero said.

"I couldn't imagine where those cattle were drinking. So I studied their trails and I found the cattle walked each day into a canyon in the mountains to drink. And then I rode back as fast as I could to tell you, señores y señorita."

"You've done well, Jaimicito. *Muchas gracias*," Ignacio said, dismissing the little vaquero.

A silence collected in the high-ceilinged room.

"Hapgood. Nathaniel Hapgood from Massachusetts—unpronounceable place. He lied to us." The eyes of the burly master of the hacienda blazed. "West of the Olivera grant, eh? That wasn't where he settled."

"I think it was only a mistake," Maria said rapidly. "They didn't deliberately lie when we stopped them. I liked the family. The man had a good, open face."

The master of the hacienda was pained by his daughter's outburst.

"Mistake or not," he growled, "they're on our grass, and we'll evict them immediately."

"Maria," the capitán said, "the gray-eyed hombre was insolent on the camino to Tucson. I've not forgotten it. Removing them will be a pleasure!"

Ignacio smiled darkly.

"First it was the Indians. Apaches! Yaqui! Papagoes! Seri! Then we fought bandidos and revolutionaries. And now, it seems, we fight the gringos. They've flooded into Tucson like wolves, ready to devour us. But they'll meet the same fate as long as I have breath in me."

The capitán was pleased. "I'll summon the pistoleros. It'll be nothing. An adventure. A few days."

The leonine patrón eyed this eager capitán of his sardonically. The man had an excess of zeal, Ignacio thought, and needed curbing.

"No hurry, my Capitán," Ignacio growled, veiling an

order in pleasantry. "Now, what do you intend to do with these Hapgoods?"

"I wish we'd leave them alone!" Maria snapped. "What harm are they? A small family. A little rancho in the mountains!"

Don Ignacio was irked. This outburst was the first he'd ever heard from his silent daughter.

"Open the door? Never, Maria. The whole pueblo of Tucson is full of these adventurers. Never!" Ignacio bristled.

"Whatever is necessary," the capitán said suavely. "If they resist, they'll die. It's happened before. You yourself have dealt severely with the Indians and all usurpers," he shrugged. "It is in *las manos de Dios.*"

"They have children!" Maria cried.

Ignacio stared at this plain daughter, this spinster who had unfortunately inherited his own beak of a nose and jowls instead of Luz's dark, dazzling refinement.

"This is men's business," he said curtly. "I will protect an inheritance the Oliveras have held since 1762 by whatever means are necessary, including death."

She held her ground. "Pedro? Will there be more shooting?"

"It will depend on the Hapgood hombre," he replied laconically. "He could choose to die bravely."

Don Ignacio enjoyed this trim capitán who had whipped his vaqueros into a peerless cavalry and had trained a cadre of pistoleros whose business it was to protect a hacienda a hundred miles long and fifteen wide.

"Maria's right but for the wrong reasons, Capitán. We are aliens here. For twenty years, since the Gadsden Purchase, I've expected trouble. Now, with their civil war over, their rabble drift west. Be careful! I care nothing about these Hapgoods, but I do care what their gobernador may think. Watch your temper!"

The capitán understood. He had been forced out of the Federales because he had failed to govern that temper; a brilliant career aborted. He smiled wanly.

"It shall be accomplished as you wish," he said, departing.

They listened to the great carved doors echo.

"He's an excellent soldado, Maria. Tomorrow he may die at Baboquivari."

She pressed her eyes closed.

He stared at her. She could not be well. She needed a husband. The last Olivera, and twenty-four. He must arrange for one before it was too late. A dowry . . .

"Maria," he said softly. "I delight in your good Christian thoughts. Mother of God, I wish it could be the way you want it. But this is the frontier, not Castile. I use methods I loathe. I do things I confess to that old padre every time he comes. Apaches! Yaqui! I put my soul in danger to defend us. I weep in confession! But I do what I must!"

She sat rigidly, listening.

An hour later the capitán clattered across the plaza with three pistoleros and reined up at the great casa.

"We're ready, Don Ignacio. Tomorrow we'll be there, soon after dawn. A little surprise."

Ignacio examined the pistoleros irritably, and the packhorses.

Gomez, color of coffee, hunter and tracker. Juanito, no surname, deadly sniper. Talliferro, the devil, unscrupulous puma, deadly with all weapons. And the capitán, schooled in all the martial arts Madrid could teach, brave and hot-tempered.

Ignacio nodded, and the four spurred their mounts north.

"Vaya con Dios, Pedro," Maria called sadly.

They trotted past the old adobe chapel and out toward

the blue spike of Baboquivari, home of the Papago gods, rising arrogantly in the north.

Early the next morning, Capitán Pedro Castillo-Armas halted before some cows branded with a large H. Their sleek calves had fresh brands.

The Hapgoods have been here only a few months, he thought. They would still be camping in that wagon, or living in a jacal. It would not be difficult to escort them to Tucson. Nonetheless . . . he would be cautious. The Norte Americanos could be fierce.

An hour later they entered the southern foothills of Baboquivari. The cattle tracks converged here at the mouth of a rising canyon. It was clear they were watering up in the mountains someplace, and grazing down here.

"Juanito—fall back, and follow behind. If we must retreat, cover us. But stay out of sight."

The mozo nodded and slowed his pony while the others moved silently forward. The capitán checked his dragoon pistol.

He would teach the Hapgoods a lesson, he thought. A lesson he wanted to spread through the streets and saloons of Tucson. One that would remind the Yankee horde who had arrived first.

The canyon walls narrowed perceptibly as the compadres climbed northward. The trail ran beside an arroyo that tumbled down the western side of the canyon.

When they rounded a gentle bend, the capitán frowned. There, in the morning shadows, was a green jewel of a meadow sloping down to a ciénaga. Sturdy mesquite corrals had some horses and a milk cow. Beyond the corrals was an adobe casa, a long rectangle with several rooms and a ramada of ocotillo poles along its front. There was also a small shed, hitch rail, well-tended garden, and a cluster of hollyhocks and marigolds at the heavy front door.

The presence of the woman complicated things, he thought. His hope of discovering a rude jacal had evaporated. This was an established rancho, built with amazing speed.

He admired the whole enterprise a moment, but then duty prompted him. These were trespassers. It was too bad for them, but they would go. And the rancho would serve the hacienda well.

A slender, well-muscled man with a pitchfork emerged from the corrals, gazing evenly toward the horsemen. He wore a pistol that sagged in an ancient holster. He jammed the pitchfork into the ground and picked up a shining rifle.

In the same instant, shutters slammed tight at the casa and the capitán caught a flash of movement at the base of the cliff beyond the ciénaga. A rifle barrel emerged from a loophole at the casa; blue metal glinted from some sort of breastwork where he had seen movement.

The capitán was irritated. There would be no surprise. It was as if these people had been expecting exactly this event and were drilled to face it. Had they been warned?

He halted his compadres and rode ahead, small and erect in his saddle. The gray-eyed gringo waited calmly a few yards from his heavy plank door.

The officer noted the Yankee's rifle. It was one of the new Winchesters, capable of spewing eighteen shots faster than he and his muchachos could fire once and reload. Insolence!

A flicker of recognition crossed the face of Nathaniel Hapgood; these men had met before. The capitán's fierce liquid brown eyes bored into the placid ones of the gringo.

"So . . ." the capitán said in English. "You lied to us after all. You are on the Olivera grant, and not on the desert to the west."

Hapgood simply didn't answer, but his alert eyes surveyed the three pistoleros one by one, weighing each. They came to rest at last on the gaunt, white-faced Talliferro, who had a bulging forehead and death written upon him.

"Are you coming to palaver or make war?" he asked at last. "If it's talk, alight and put your horses in the corral yonder. If it's war, show your colors and face what comes."

Insolent! thought the capitán. This New Englander was going to cause trouble. One grown man, a farmer; his muchacho over there above the ciénaga; and the woman inside . . . against experienced pistoleros. He smiled blandly.

"You try my patience, Señor Hapgood."

"Look—I've no stomach for trouble, Señor—Señor . . . ?"

"Capitán. Capitán Castillo-Armas."

". . . Capitán. I'd like to talk to Olivera. I'll go over there, or invite him here, and we can settle this peaceably. In fact, if he can show me that we're on his land, why, we could settle with him. . . . Surely he'll not mind having a neighbor once we chew the fat a little."

Hapgood smiled amiably at the man above him on the horse.

Insolent! The Yankee was making himself the equal of his patrón whose land stretched leagues and leagues into Arizona and Sonora!

"His orders are to remove you to Tucson immediately, and we will proceed at once," said Castillo-Armas icily. "You are trespassing."

"Well I don't know about that," said Hapgood quietly. "You brought documents proving that? There's no such records on file with the authorities. Only my homestead claim."

"*Bastante!* Enough!" the capitán spat. "We defend

what is ours." He didn't like being forced to the defensive.

"So I've heard," said Hapgood laconically. "And also what's not yours."

The capitán rose erect in his saddle, a gesture full of proud menace. "This is my last warning. You will surrender your weapons and go peaceably. If not—" He smiled suddenly, in truth anticipating what might come.

Nathaniel Hapgood sighed, not liking the direction events were taking, or the mounting jeopardy to Patience, Jonathan, and Charity. He had been warned about the Oliveras. Warned that men never returned, that whole families disappeared. He had scoffed, but now some queasy feeling told him it was true.

"Surrender or die. Is that it?" he asked.

"Enough talk. Put down that rifle and you won't be harmed. And tell the others."

The capitán was not worried about the octagonal barrel emerging from the loophole: women wouldn't shoot. But the muchacho, fifty yards off, was another matter.

Hapgood gazed at his home, built with grueling work in this desert wilderness. And the corrals, the adobe shed, the fences, the garden. And then at the tawny ridges that cupped this canyon home between them.

"I think not. This Winchester's the only friend I've got here, seems like." He cradled the weapon loosely. The slightest turn—a few degrees—would bring it to bear on the mestizo to the left, who sat impassively on his pony.

Anger blazed in the capitán, and he slid his dragoon pistol down upon Hapgood in one smooth motion. Then the capitán raised the bleak black barrel level with Nathaniel's eyes.

"For God's sake, Nathaniel," cried Patience softly from within. He heard her, but watched him.

Some terrible force solidified in the New Englander, and he stubbornly froze and waited. Moments passed.

"You see? You don't wish to kill in cold blood," he said softly. "You'd only have to kill the rest—the women—to keep the silence. You don't wish to kill little girls."

It was true. The capitán had killed often enough in war, and in Federale raids on bandidos. But not like this. The capitán's eyes bored steadily into the Yankee's, almost physically driving him back.

But strangely, Hapgood stepped one pace forward instead. And then another.

"Enough!" snapped the soldier.

The pasty, odd rider on the right, the one Hapgood really feared, watched intently, missing nothing, hands resting on the saddle horn. Hapgood knew somehow the man could put a knife or bullet into him faster than he could swing his rifle there.

The capitán walked his gelding into Hapgood, until the pistol was only inches from the New Englander's face.

"Pa . . . are you all right? Pa! Tell me . . ." The youthful voice of Hapgood's son drifted down from the stronghold at the cliff, seeking direction.

Nathaniel Hapgood didn't reply. In fact he had ceased thinking moments before, and there was only a pulsing animal will to survive in him, a naked clash of will power with the man on the horse above him. A tremor shook the capitán, and the muscles bulged around his mouth.

Inside the gloomy casa, Patience Hapgood was speechless with terror. She closed her eyes. Her old Sharps sagged, and the gaunt Talliferro noticed.

Nathaniel stepped forward again, hard against the horse's withers, closer still to the pistol. Involuntarily the capitán yanked back his arm, the reaction of a man burned, and with the spasm there came to him the recognition of a superior will, some sheer force. And, simultaneously, a Latin rage.

"*Bastante!*" he roared, spurring the horse with his cruel star rowels. The animal slammed into Hapgood, bowling him backward. He staggered, careened a dozen feet out of balance, and stumbled into rocky earth. The Winchester clattered away, far away.

Jonathan Hapgood didn't shoot. There was nothing to shoot at.

All the demons of bad temper were loosed in the officer. He had been backed down by some mad force beyond courage, some summoning of faith beyond will. He felt defeated without knowing why and now he fired wildly at this tumbling Yankee, hitting nothing, spitting up adobe. He uncoiled the bullwhip and now, insanely, snapped the whistling plaited rawhide down upon the gringo. It hit Hapgood with the crack of a rifle shot, and Patience Hapgood screamed from within.

A stripe of blood oozed across Hapgood's back. Another crack swung him around and lifted him off the dirt. A third lash brought blood to his chest. More explosive cracks brought Hapgood to his knees and he clawed blindly away from the howling whip. Hapgood's back turned sheet red as the weighted tassel sliced his blue shirt to shreds.

The boy at the ciénaga fired, and the whistling bullet brought instant calm to the enraged capitán. Another shot plucked the bullwhip from him and barely missed his hand. He whirled the gelding, waved to his compadres, and the three horsemen stormed toward the cliffside redoubt. Hapgood collapsed to the earth in agony.

From her loophole within, Patience Hapgood fired the Sharps buffalo gun at the third horseman, the pale one with the bulbous forehead. The recoil knocked her backward but the huge lead ball creased the rump of the horse, and it began bucking violently. She saw the pale man yank the reins savagely and then dismount with a catlike leap that placed him behind the shielding animal.

She raced outside to Hapgood and drew the Navy Colt from his holster and emptied it at the man behind the horse.

"Nathaniel!" she cried as she plunged down beside him. He moaned incoherently. She lifted him tenderly and began to drag him toward the casa, scarcely aware of the shots and shouts that were piercing the silence of the canyon.

She dragged him a few feet, but he was heavy. Then she found strength to pull him ten feet more. He recovered his senses enough to crawl while she dragged him, panting, using strength she didn't know she had.

Then the shooting stopped and there was a terrible silence.

She pulled desperately. The New Englander moved into the threshold of the casa where there could be safety for a while. Then he lunged all the way in.

"Do not move. Stand up. Both of you," rasped the metallic voice of the capitán above them. Patience stared upward into the furious eyes of the soldier, and then at the black pistol pointing down at her.

Beyond, she saw her son, tear-stained, hands tied cruelly behind him—but alive and unhurt. The twelve-year-old had fought bravely against seasoned pistoleros.

Hapgood summoned all his will power to stand, but collapsed in a heap when he tried to rise off his knees.

"Stand up or die." The capitán smiled evilly.

Hapgood stood then, while Patience bore his dead weight. Only his fear that the pistol in the hand of his tormentor would explode upon them all gave him the strength to stand.

The little girl, Charity, clung weepily to her mother's skirts and was stained with her father's blood.

"You are lucky to be alive," said the capitán. "We will now escort you to Tucson."

"My husband's in no condition for a two-day journey!" Patience snapped.

"He should have considered that before all this—this insolence!" the capitán retorted. "We will go. If he doesn't survive—" The capitán shrugged his shoulders. "You have one hour."

"What about our cattle?" Hapgood rasped.

"We'll round them up," replied the capitán. "One half we will keep to pay for the grass they've eaten. The other will be returned at our leisure—if they are yours."

"And my house? Are you going to send along half of that? And the corrals? And the shed? And my freight wagon and mule team?" Nathaniel asked hotly.

"It all belongs to the patrón," said Castillo-Armas blandly.

A fury boiled up in the New Englander, only to subside in a wave of pain and weakness.

"You will take nothing. Saddle your horses and be grateful you aren't walking," the capitán added.

Gomez gathered the Winchesters, the Colt, and the Sharps and stacked them in a corner, while watching the gringo family with narrow eyes. The pale Talliferro skulked outside, missing nothing, eying everything.

There was no time; no time at all. Patience stared crazily at the family tintypes. She wanted a shawl. She wanted her wedding dress in the trunk. She wanted . . . her eyes blurred. Nathaniel groaned, and she began to wash and bind his wounds.

Hapgood stared at the home he had built. Waves of pain descended and lifted, and he couldn't focus his eyes during the worst moments. His heart sank. There was love here, and an enterprise with promise. Oh, God, why?

He rose at last, and painfully threw a saddle on a gelding Jonathan brought him. The more he struggled with the saddles, the more bearable was his pain, and by the time four horses were readied he knew he could endure the trip.

Patience was not given to public display of emotions—it was something ingrained from her Puritan heritage—so she held back her tears and pressed her lips until her jaw was white. There was one thing she was going to take, no matter what they said—the family Bible. It had been owned by the Hapgoods ever since they arrived at the Massachusetts Bay Colony in 1634; on its foreleaf there were recorded, in several hands, the births, marriages, and deaths of ten generations. She reached for it and clutched it to her breast.

"Nothing!" snapped the capitán. "Gomez—"

The mestizo wrenched it from her. Castillo-Armas was immediately sorry, but he was a proud man and he could not possibly recant before this family. He was sorry, and it was something he would remember to confess to the padre when next he came to the hacienda.

Patience stared at him blackly. Her fears and tears had been transformed into the most intense calm she had ever felt. She stared unblinkingly at the capitán then, saying more with those frightful eyes than a thousand words would say. The capitán looked away and cursed.

At last they filed silently down the canyon, and Nathaniel looked unhappily at his mules and freight wagon. He had paid three hundred dollars for the outfit and it was something that could support them until—until they returned home. As he planned to do. Even if it killed him.

Talliferro eyed the mules and wagon contemplatively. They would fetch much in Hermosillo. The mare and foal, too. And everything in the casa. He would have to slip back quickly, before it was all turned over to the patrón.

His shaded eyes watched Patience, and then sized up the hombre. Hapgood was brave, but he would die easily if it came to that: a farmer, merely, unfamiliar with the arts of violence.

Talliferro attributed his survival and his prowess to his powers of observation. He alone had noticed the trail northward up the canyon. He would take it soon. And he alone had counted the cattle and calculated the wealth here, free for the taking.

Down the canyon, Juanito emerged from cover, and the capitán ordered him to stay at the Hapgood casa until some vaqueros could be sent. When the silent party reached the rincon, the capitán dispatched Talliferro to report to Don Ignacio.

Then the party moved swiftly north, and a deadly quiet was upon them. That night the air was cold through Nathaniel's shredded shirt. He fell into a heavy sleep on the sand, and Patience pressed herself to him to keep him warm and share her love. But it was she who drew comfort, finding his grasp warm and strong.

She slipped her hand to the forehead of her man, and found him fevered.

"Bloody but unbowed." He grinned. "We'll be back."

She turned away unhappily. She didn't want to return. "Hush!" she whispered. "We won't make plans until you're well. Oh, darling . . ." she sighed in the darkness.

In the morning Nathaniel was weaker, and had to hold the saddle horn with both hands. The sun blistered his wounds through the shredded shirt. He was too tired to be hungry. So was Patience, but the children whimpered.

The capitán knew better than to speak, but he passed the canteen often, and rested frequently. He was a soldier and had seen hard things.

When the shadows were long, he led them down the long slope into the hot valley of Tucson, and drew up before the long, low, adobe façade of the Santa Rita Hotel.

"If you return to Baboquivari, a much worse fate will befall you," he warned.

Nathaniel and Patience stared. The capitán and Gomez rode across the plaza to the part of town where the tongue was Spanish.

Nathaniel eased off his mount and Jonathan wordlessly led the horses to the livery. There was time for Patience to withdraw money at the bank where they had dealings. . . . By sundown they had rooms, had bathed and eaten, and had fallen into an oblivion of sleep.

"We did it," Nathaniel mumbled as he drifted off.

"Did what?"

"Went to Baboquivari and came out alive."

CHAPTER 2

In the summer of 1873 Nathaniel Hapgood laid plans to homestead a ranch in the desert mountains southwest of Tucson. It was a land little known—and carefully guarded.

He prodded his eleven-year-old son across the plaza of the pueblo, sleepy in the afternoon sun.

"They'll probably be having a siesta," he grumbled. "The desert heat gets to Anglos worse than the Mexicans."

He steered the boy into a long low building with three-foot adobe walls barricading the fierce heat. Twenty years earlier it had housed the alcalde along with a garrison of his soldados. Now the stars and stripes hung limply in the dusty air, and the place was occupied by the territorial clerk.

The jarring door awakened a dozing, muttonchopped functionary.

"I'm filing a homestead claim in the Baboquivaris—nice canyon down there," Nathaniel explained. "I'd like a section map and whatever else I'll need."

"Baboquivaris?" the bulbous clerk yawned. "Forget it. The Oliveras have all that country on the Altar Valley side of those mountains, and the government's fixing to reserve the country west of the mountains for the Papagoes. And there ain't a decent map of the area anyway."

"I'd like to see the Olivera grant," Nathaniel persisted.
"That Spanish crown grant may not reach where I'm
going. The place I'm eying is a long canyon right in those
mountains. It's got a good ciénaga on it, a grassy flat, and
plenty of graze above. I'd like to patent the ciénaga and
the head of the canyon, and squat on the grazing land
above until I can prove it up."

The clerk drummed his fingers on the counter. "Those
Oliveras never recorded that grant with us. Never had the
need, I guess. You'd have to wander down to Hermosillo,
in Sonora, to get those boundaries. . . . All we know is
that the crown gave 'em the hull Altar Valley, clean down
to Caborca and almost up to here. They were supposed to
register it with us within four years of the purchase, but
they never did. Fact is, very few Mex ever did."

"That's not much help," Nathaniel said. "Let's see your
maps."

The clerk unrolled an old military map. In the gloom of
the rear office a dark young man with high cheekbones
lifted his eyes from his ledgers to stare at Hapgood.

"Funny," Hapgood mused. "That canyon doesn't even
show on here. It starts here in the rincon and runs sort of
north to the base of the peak."

He was irked. No map. No boundaries. No Olivera
claim.

"We'll go squat, then," he said, annoyed.

"Mister, I'm telling you plain," said the clerk. "The
ones that go there don't come back. That's Olivera country. Olivera's a Mex patriot. He was Santa Anna's adjutant. Governor of Sonora once. He's got an army of pistoleros that are handy with the Indians and bandits. The
Mex flag flies over his hacienda even though it's on our
side. I don't know how you got in and out of those moun-

tains alive, but you were plain lucky. Better not push that luck."

The bookkeeper stared intently at Nathaniel.

The New Englander sighed. "I've been in there three times," he said. "These things get built up out of proportion. I'll palaver with the Oliveras if I have to. There's never been a man I couldn't come to an agreement with, though sometimes I have to show them the lay of it."

The clerk shook his head.

"Suit yourself. But don't expect the territory to back your play. Have you ever seen Olivera shopping in the pueblo here? He's got more armor than an armadillo."

"I like that canyon," said Nathaniel mildly. "The ciénaga's got sweet water. Grass up to my belly. I'll claim what I can. Gotta pen?"

For fifteen minutes the office was silent, save for the scratching. He chose the words carefully, laying claim to the water and canyon, and the graze clear down to the border. Then he signed, and dated it 3 September 1873.

"Worthless piece of paper," the clerk grumbled. "But I'll file it. The date might help—if you live."

The Yankee and his son emerged into the blinding light, and trudged down an alley toward a gunsmith he knew about, across the adobe street from the Butterfield Stage.

"The boy and I want identical repeating rifles if the price is right," Nathaniel explained. "Maybe some Henrys."

Jasper Wiggin lifted his stovepipe hat and settled it glumly over his bald head. He was not a man to be pushed into a sale if he could help it.

"Maybe I got some, maybe I don't," he grumbled. "My price is high and I double it for dudes. And you don't want Henrys. They ain't made anymore."

"Okay," said Nathaniel, "show us what you've got."

"Winchester bought the patents in 1871 and put their name on the Henrys. Same gun, new name."

"Well, let's have a lookee at the Winchesters then," said the Yankee impatiently.

"I ain't going to sell 'em to you," Wiggin retorted. "That line's been discontinued. Now they got a new one, lever-action, forty-four–forty repeater. Magazine long as the barrel. Holds seventeen cartridges and you can fire fast as you can lever. But I don't think I'll sell 'em to you."

"Then you won't get my double eagles," Nathaniel said.

"I sell it to drovers and the like who've got kissing relationships with the Apaches," said Wiggin triumphantly. "Say, did you say gold?"

Nathaniel hefted the weapon and liked it. He levered an imaginary cartridge into the chamber and drew a bead on the whale-oil lamp.

"Yes, but not for you. You're going to take greenbacks and like it," said Nathaniel.

"Well they ain't for sale to you buzzards." Wiggin grinned maliciously.

"What's the price in double eagles?"

"Gold? Aw . . ." Wiggin struggled with himself. "List price is thirty-four dollars. Sixty-eight each for dudes."

"Now, Wiggin, that price is well nigh blasphemy," Nathaniel retorted. "We'll want some protection out in the Papago country."

"Papago country! Why, why, you could defend yourself with a flintlock and a dull kitchen knife out there," Wiggin snorted.

"Pa, let's go to another gunsmith," Jonathan pleaded. "He's trying to schnooker us."

"Son, there never was a man I couldn't deal with. Even this bandit here," Nathaniel replied.

"Seventy-five each!" Wiggin snarled.

"Actually, Wiggin, we're settling next to the Olivera grant. I'd feel plain naked without these repeaters."

"*Olivera?*" The gunsmith sighed glumly. "I'll have to sell, then. Thirty dollars in gold. In advance. No one going to Olivera country's got credit with me."

"I thought you'd be reasonable," Nathaniel drawled. "Now, how about a thousand forty-four–forty cartridges?"

He rolled the double eagles out of his bag.

"You'd better take two thousand if you're going into that country," Wiggin snapped. He picked up the coins and methodically bit them. "Don't see much gold . . .

"Say," he added, "want me to show you which end the bullet comes out of?"

"We'll figure it out. Where're you from, Wiggin?"

"New York, the Empire State."

"Thought so," Nathaniel snapped. "Crookedest state in the union."

"It was until I moved here," Wiggin roared. "And now Arizona Territory is. Get out! Don't expect no service!"

Nathaniel prodded the boy west, toward the freight depot on the Santa Cruz. "Better stop swinging those rifles around. People might take fright," he grumbled. "One more stop, and then we'll walk home."

He found the freight rig that had been advertised, but the price was too high. No self-respecting Yankee would pay four hundred dollars for a beat-up rig like that, he thought.

He circled the wagon again and liked it. Solid oak, with plank walls that veed up from the bed to the height of a man. Good iron tires, but three cracked spokes. Hubs in good shape; axles and springs tolerably good. Cracked tongue. Harness worn.

The trouble was with the mule team. Those hoofs . . .

"I'll give three hundred for it," Nathaniel allowed, addressing the teamster.

"No suh," the giant southerner replied. "These here freighters are rare as snow in Sonora and one rig like this will make a man right prosperous."

Nathaniel squinted at the truculent teamster in the glaring sun.

"Well," he drawled, "I like those mules well enough. Big fellers. Looks like they were sired by a giant jack on Percheron mares. Trouble is, their feet are plumb bad."

The teamster looked uneasily at the slender gray-eyed Yankee.

"Yes," Nathaniel continued, "I can understand why you're wanting to unload this rig so all-fired fast. Three of those eight mules got sand cracks in the hoofs so bad they need a six-month vacation. That paste and bootblack you fancied up those hoofs with sure had me buffaloed for a few minutes."

"Wall, now, I've got lotsa gents looking at the rig," the teamster responded defensively.

"Sure you do. It's the only freight outfit for sale in the pueblo. Traces are shot and it's hauled too much silver ore . . ."

"You ain't buyin' it new."

"What do you think, Jonathan?" Nathaniel asked.

"It sure is big, Pa. Twice as big as those Conestoga wagons."

"Three hundred in double eagles," Nathaniel said. "And not a peso more. It'll take me six months to get those hoofs in shape."

"Double eagles?" The teamster's truculence evaporated. "Gold? I didn't know there was that much gold in Arizona Territory. Them greenbacks are all you ever see, and you've got to spend them the day you get 'em or else you're stuck. . . . Now, mister, it's a deal."

Nathaniel dropped fifteen gold coins into the hands of the seller, and tucked the bill of sale in his pocket. He stopped at the livery office on the way out.

"I bought that rig," he said to George Overmeier. "Can your smithy do some repairs?"

"Anything you want," the proprietor said.

"Three new spokes, new tongue, new plank in the tail-gate. All hardwood or you won't get a tin peso out of me. Also I want some hardwood bows and canvas over the top, waterproof. And you'd better rivet some leather on those traces."

"That's quite an order."

"You'll get a pair of double eagles for it. I'll want it in a week."

"Where you going in such a rush?" asked Overmeier.

"I've a claim over in the Baboquivaris, west of Olivera."

The manager paled. "You're crazy," he said. "You'll either die or become Olivera's son-in-law."

Nathaniel Hapgood grinned.

It was settled then, and Nathaniel guided his stripling son home.

"It'll get us there, Jon. One more trip won't hurt those bad hoofs much more, and then they can rest."

Jonathan had a time of it keeping up with his long-striding father through the pueblo.

"A feller tried that one on me at Concord. That slicker was from Boston and he rode into our farm leading a right fancy mare for sale. But I saw where he'd patched a cracked foot with oakum or tar or something, and I said, 'Sir, I'm a subscriber to the Golden Rule and I'm going to do to you ex-zactly as I'd want to be done to,' and I picked up my pitchfork and ran him halfway to Lexington."

Nathaniel exploded with laughter.

They walked silently beside walls that radiated the sun's violent heat, past grilled windows, the casas and cocinas of mahogany people. Alkali dust powdered their faces and throats. The desert town was stirring again in the sinking sun. The Hapgoods passed burdened burros and clattering wagons.

"I did what I could. There's not much law in the territory, but I got what there is of it on my side."

"These lever actions will be all the law we need where we're going," the boy said proudly.

"Son, I mightily hope not!" Nathaniel exploded. "You just haven't seen much dying, the way I did in the First Massachusetts. No, I'm hoping to have a good palaver with Olivera. I figure most men are reasonable enough. They just get riled up when people start pushing. Anyway, we're Yankees, boy, and whoever heard of a Yank who couldn't talk his way into something?"

They turned into a quiet clay street, walled by adobe homes.

"I don't think Ma wants to go out there," the boy said.

Nathaniel sighed. "Tucson's a pleasant place for her. She's had Concepcion keeping house, too. She likes to be with people, that's all. That was the way of it back in Concord, before the doctors told her she had consumption."

"They sure were wrong," the boy said stoutly.

"They sure were, and thank God for that. Six months to live, my eye! That was nothing but a deep chest cold, but they sure uprooted us to get her out here."

"Once she puts her mind to it, she'll like living in the canyon," the boy said.

They entered the cool parlor, which faced upon the dusty street. Nathaniel watched Patience rise in the cloistered quiet. Her tall elegance mellowed him, as it always did. She was slender and erect, with large Wedgwood-blue eyes in an oval face. Her glossy brown hair was sometimes worn in a bun, but today it hung in two large curls over her breast.

She smiled as she watched Jonathan stack the rifles in a corner, and lower the heavy cartridge boxes, and then there was a questioning in her tranquil eyes.

Nathaniel slid an arm about her. "We're going," he said.

She was silent.

"We can leave in a week or so."

"You know how I feel about it," she replied.

"Yup, but you've got the misfortune of loving a roving man." He grinned.

She laughed. She always did when she needed to. And she squeezed his hand.

"I skinned that teamster out of his wagon, filed a claim on the canyon, and picked up the artillery. Lever actions."

"I thought you promised the Papago country would be safe."

"The best life is rarely safe," he replied.

"Well, you'd better show me how to shoot one! . . . Jonathan, go help Charity set the table."

The boy scurried to the kitchen.

She hugged her man, the only man in the world who could lure her into an Arizona wilderness.

"I'll miss it here. Concepcion and her gossip. And all the fun. I love this pueblo; it's so different from home. Do you know what that crazy Pepito did when he brought ice? He led that burro of his right into my kitchen! I told him he was loco."

She laughed happily and hugged Nathaniel tight.

During the next days she packed china and silver and her good dresses into barrels while Nathaniel bought cattle, dickered for saddle horses, and gathered mounds of supplies. The barrels of finery would have to stay in Tucson for the time being, but she rebelled at the thought of a totally drab wilderness home and packed "a trunk of sillies" —as she called it—just for herself. Into it went tintypes of her parents, a hand mirror, brushes, scented soap, sewing things, and her wedding dress.

Then one evening she hugged Concepcion tearfully, already missing the vivacious Mexican girl who had been one of the family for almost a year. The next cool September dawn the big brown mules hunkered into their harness and the burdened freight wagon rumbled south through the hushed streets of the pueblo. Jonathan rode on a steel-dust gelding bought from a haggling Texan, and led two others.

"You'll be able to handle it," Nathaniel assured the woman beside him. He flicked the eight reins gathered in his big fists, and the mules danced into a fast trot.

"It's no more trouble than driving the buckboard with our matched Morgans back home. 'Cept these brakes take some manhandling to slow her down. But Jon or I can always hop up here to lend a hand."

"Oh, I'll make the best teamster you ever hired." Patience smiled. "I learned all the words coming to Santa Fe, and I just might try some as long as I'm pioneering."

The New Englander stared oddly at his wife.

She tucked a blanket tight around her sleeping little girl.

"Charity's just a mite of a child, but I'll be putting her on one of those cutting horses," he said. "All she has to do is hang on. The horse will know what to do."

They reached their herd, pastured on the west bank of the Santa Cruz, about the time the morning sun was gleaming from the white towers of San Xavier del Bac, in the hazy south. Nathaniel paid the two Papago vaqueros, and then lifted Charity gently onto the back of a big buckskin.

"Just hang on to the horn, honey. The horse knows what to do and he'll chase those cows back into the herd. You can go back to sleep in the wagon after we get the herd trailed out."

Nathaniel howled at a hundred and ten cows, bred heifers, bulls, and spare horses until the sluggish mass of beef began drifting west and slowly lined out into a trail string.

"Har, har, har," Patience yelled, and the urbane mules rotated their ears back to catch more of the feminine novelty. She cracked the bullwhip, and that was authority they knew, and they pressed into their collars until the heavy wagon creaked forward along the Ajo Road.

"Git along you sons of bitches," she roared, thinking the men were far forward. But from the corner of her eye she saw her son through the dust, her dear Jonathan, gaping at her.

She laughed.

They nooned in the creosote bush flats north of the Sierrita Mountains, and far off to the southwest, across the Altar Valley, they could see the blue spike of Baboquivari looming two thousand feet above the rest of the western rampart. Even from that fifty-mile distance the peak was awesome and foreboding. Patience shivered. Far to the west she saw dust being stirred by the passage of several horsemen and perhaps a wagon.

"Beyond the peak, coming up from the south, is our canyon," Nathaniel said softly as if to read her thoughts. "There's curving ridges on either side, coming out from Baboquivari like the arms of the Sphinx," he said. "We'll be settling right between them, comfortable as cubs between a lion's paws."

She stared uncertainly toward the mysterious blue mountain.

"Wait till you see it!" he exclaimed. "With that tan rock rising up north of us and the green bunch-grass meadow below. And the ciénaga! Most likely an acre of it, cattails and all right there in the desert, trapped by a rock ledge and fed by sweet water. There's timber above, too, real timber, piñon pine, not mesquite, popping out of every crack in the face of that mountain. Papagoes say their god, Elder Brother, lives up on top, and all the rest of their spirits, and it's easy to see why they think it."

She smiled at him, loving his enthusiasm and vitality.

The eastbound party drew closer, stirring up a towering cloud of amber dust. There was a wagon and at least four riders moving leisurely along the hot road.

"Jonathan, let's get rolling," Nathaniel said uneasily. They prodded the reluctant herd until it once again began its sinuous flow westward. Patience bullied the sweat-caked mules until the iron tires sang again upon the earth.

They watched a phaeton draw close, pulled by spirited white horses. A compact man in a starched white suit was driving, and beside him a dark woman in creamy linen sat erectly under a parasol. There were four armed outriders, their faces shaded by large sombreros. They were carrying carbines and pistols. As the distance closed, the approaching party hewed unwaveringly to the twin-rut road, and Nathaniel wondered whether they were going to collide with the herd.

He galloped forward and prodded the herd right, even as Patience pulled fistfuls of reins until the wagon eased out of the ruts and onto the desert. She planted her feet and hauled on the brakes until movement died.

The driver of the phaeton stopped beside Patience. He was a small, leonine man with iron-gray hair jutting electrically outward. He stared silently at the Hapgoods, but the young woman beside him smiled, and looked sympathetically up toward Patience.

The three pistoleros stared at the cattle and the freshly burned H upon their thighs. The fourth, a slender, mustachioed man in an officer's tunic, rode forward to Nathaniel and nodded slightly while his liquid brown eyes surveyed them all.

"Who might you be, señor?" he asked in accented English.

"Hapgood. Nathaniel Hapgood from Massachusetts," was the laconic response.

"Where might you be going, señor?"

"Can't rightly say that's your business," Nathaniel replied.

"We make it our business," the officer responded coldly.

Nathaniel glanced at the leonine man in the phaeton, and realized he was following the English conversation perfectly.

"Wherever we're going, we'll be west of the Olivera holdings," Nathaniel said, and was satisfied to see the older man's eyes narrow.

The bronzed pistoleros stood still, understanding nothing. But there was an odd one, a pasty-skinned skeletal one with darting eyes who made Nathaniel's flesh crawl.

"We'll be moving along then," said Nathaniel, and he spurred his heavy gelding into the herd. Jonathan boogered the cattle and Patience whipped the mules while the others watched silently. In a few minutes a mile separated the groups.

"I didn't like the way that went at all," Nathaniel grumbled. "That military fellow riled me with his tone of voice. And they could have pulled off for our herd."

He rode silently beside Patience awhile.

"That was old Ignacio himself, and his daughter I suppose. And those were tough hombres. But you know what? They're a mite smaller than they were made out to be in Tucson."

Nathaniel spurred his big bay forward, leaving Patience to her worries. She stared at the quiet girl beside her, so trusting in her childish way. And then she remembered that strange, pasty-white pistolero with the darting eyes, and she felt a nameless dread, a foreboding she had experienced ever since she saw Baboquivari for the first time, before lunch.

CHAPTER 3

Patience let the reins hang limply while she gaped from her wagon seat at her new home.

The greedy cattle gulped the water of the ciénaga and then drifted out upon the belly-high grass.

It was all Nathaniel had said. Baboquivari jutted so high above that she had to throw back her head to look into its upper reaches. She was in a park of perhaps fifty acres, all of it verdant grass watered by summer showers the benevolent peak wrung from the reluctant desert skies. To either side were tawny ridges, a jumble of prickly pear, ocotillo, saguaro, cholla, and mesquite. They guarded the intimate valley and set boundaries upon her new home.

She felt lonely here amid the grandeur, and for a fleeting moment she remembered the young woman in the phaeton, Maria Louisa Olivera—her nearest neighbor —and she wished friendship were possible. But it would never be.

She dropped down from the wagon and walked toward the ciénaga, aware that Nathaniel was watching her anxiously. She stirred up a flock of red-winged blackbirds from the cattails and brought silence to the little oasis.

"I'll want to put in a garden today," she said quietly. "Perhaps we'll have a few things before frost."

He took her hand, wanting to share with her his love of this eden.

"I thought to build a house on the high ground here, away from the arroyo," he said earnestly. "With windows opening out upon the peak and ridges, and a front door facing down the canyon, where our guests will come."

"What guests?" she asked somberly.

He was saddened then, and the exhilaration of arriving to claim his promised land seeped out of his spirit.

"The house'll have to wait a bit," he sighed. "First thing is to get these cattle up into the mountains onto summer pasture. There's lots of *tanques* and *tinajas* up there from the showers, and the grass will be high. If the cattle can scramble around those slopes, they'll make a living."

"Hey, Pa, I found a fort," yelled Jonathan. He was standing in a hollowed area beneath an overhanging cliff above the spring. Rock talus from the façade above had formed a ragged breastwork in front.

"Why, so you have, son," Nathaniel agreed as he examined the place. It was indeed a stronghold, commanding the park and southern reaches of the canyon.

"Bring the old Sharps over, son. Wrap it in oilcloth. We'll store some powder, water, and jerky here too. I don't know a parcel about defense, but I reckoned I picked up a few things in the infantry. I can improve this with a few logs. . . ."

They unloaded the wagon and made a snug home of it under the canvas-covered bows. It would protect them until they had enough adobe bricks for a house.

Tomorrow would begin months of grueling work that would result in a house, outbuildings, corrals, and a garden. Nathaniel's plan was simply to build as fast as possible. When the inevitable day of discovery came, the Oliveras would discover a functioning ranch rather than a camp. He doubted the Oliveras would destroy something solid, something established.

The next dawn, Nathaniel and Jonathan saddled the bay and baldface and herded the cattle up a steep deer trail that rose from the head of the canyon to the high country. They discovered a rocky plateau far above, covered with full tinajas, and released the cattle there. Then they explored craggy slopes where the piñon grew, looking for springs and seeps. As they worked east they struck a great dike of volcanic rock that formed a natural barrier between their pasture and the long ridges leading down to the Altar Valley.

The father and son began work on the corrals. They planted pairs of upright posts and then laid mesquite limbs between them in the fashion of the country. They finished two sturdy pens, with gates that swung on rawhide, and then began making adobe bricks.

They scythed the native grasses for hay, and forked it into a great stack. Some days they harnessed two mules and dragged piñon logs down from the high slopes, logs that would be squared into vigas, or beams, for their casa.

As the days passed, the adobe dust eddied into their tracks across the Altar Valley, and dust devils filled their prints. The sun baked the scourings of their cattle. The summer showers pummeled the sand, until nothing remained of their passage and the wilderness swallowed them up.

The days grew shorter and cooler, and it was time to build a house against the cold. Nathaniel fashioned window frames and a door and shutters from his small hoard of sawn wood. Beams were squared for lintels.

"Tomorrow we'll start," he announced. "Everyone will help. Jon, you'll haul brick. Patience will mix adobe in buckets, and I'll lay up the bricks. Charity, you'll bring us lots of cool water and do other things, like a big girl."

It took only two days to complete the walls of the first room, and before a week passed the walls of three rooms stood: a central kitchen and living room, a bedroom for the children, and another for Nathaniel and Patience.

With the help of the mules they dragged the heavy vigas up over the walls and laid skinned poles on them, then straw matting and adobe clay. Nathaniel hung heavy shutters and doors, and cut small loopholes in them for defense. The sawn wood was thick enough to stop bullets and arrows and cold.

They moved in and rejoiced. Later they would cover the dirt floors with sandstone or plank, and replace the rawhide hinges with iron. And Nathaniel planned a ramada along the southern side for shade. But there was no time for that. The nights grew cold and he rustled firewood while Patience harvested what she could from the frosted garden.

Some days, Nathaniel felt cloistered, and then he saddled his bay, the one he called Cotton Mather, and rode south to the mouth of the canyon, and stared out upon the rincon for signs of life or danger: cattle, Olivera vaqueros, Indians—anything.

He never saw movement. The Olivera grant was vast, and much of it useless except when it rained and the vaqueros could water cattle from local arroyos and tanques. He suspected there were broad reaches which no Olivera hombre had seen for years. And yet he watched, dreading the day when men would come into his mountain refuge.

Jonathan mastered the horses as well as the Winchesters, and began bringing home venison tied to the back of the baldface—the only horse that would tolerate that sort of burden.

High upon a ridge he discovered the skeleton of a calf, and knew the pumas had feasted. He searched the slopes and found the whitened bones of two cows and four more calves. But he spotted groups of live cattle as well, which had grown wily and broke from him like deer.

The news appalled Nathaniel. The next day he and the boy rode the high country and were sickened to discover at least twenty skeletons. The mountain was a Moloch, devouring their very livelihood. They had unwittingly donated their little herd to the mountain lions.

But they noted the live longhorns had grown cagey and shy. Dozens of them appeared on the high slopes, and among them were new calves.

They hunted the puma through the short days of November, but rarely saw a cat and never had a target. They hid near a fresh kill for two days, but the lions never returned. The slaughter continued, even while the father and son hunted the pumas, and by the end of the year Nathaniel was sure that half his herd had been devoured.

He began to sense defeat: the pumas, rather than the Oliveras, were steadily ruining his little ranch.

Patience wasn't happy, but her days were made tolerable by unending toil. She worked mechanically to turn the casa into a home. She gathered wild herbs and spices. She pulled the family tintypes from her trunk and displayed them. She found time to fill a vase with the last of the fall flowers.

The family rested only upon the sabbath, when Nathaniel opened the big family Bible and read a passage of scripture. But that day of enforced idleness was all the harder for Patience, and she came to dread the empty hours when there was neither work nor friends.

She began to take long walks down the canyon to the broad rincon on Sunday afternoons.

"I wish you'd take the old Colt with you," Nathaniel said unhappily.

"No. It's heavy. And we've never had a bit of trouble," she replied irritably.

Neither of them knew that on several occasions obsidian eyes high upon the western shoulder of Baboquivari had watched her slow progress south; had observed her yearning glances out upon the open prairie, and had watched her dejected return up the canyon.

One raw January morning Nathaniel rode west along Baboquivari's shoulder into new country. The peak vaulted upward so straight that he couldn't see the top. At the foot of the façade was a steep talus-laden slope that was difficult for the bay to pick through.

But he found cattle sign, so he eased the mount through the rubble, past the scrubby piñon, and north. The sign led relentlessly upward to the creamy volcanic massif of the peak. He spotted a great slab of stone that had cracked loose from the sheer cliff eons before, and embedded itself at the apex of the western shoulder. And it was there that the sign led Nathaniel.

He eased the bay into a narrow defile between the slab and the mountain, and discovered an eerie cave lined with volcanic glass. Some vast age before, it had been a bubble in the molten lava and had hardened into a chamber that sank down gently from its opening.

Nathaniel dismounted and led the spooky gelding in. There were fresh droppings, and at the rear he found a black pool of cold water that apparently had drained into the cave as it rushed down the face of the sacred mountain.

Smoke curled from a tiny fire, the size of a man's hand, and for a moment Nathaniel was paralyzed. Someone had been there only moments before! Then in the gloom he saw Indian paintings, and on high shelves he found totems and beads. It was a sacred place of the Papagoes, he suspected. Perhaps even the home of Elder Brother. He clutched his Colt nervously.

He realized the cave offered refuge from rain, cold, thirst—or pistoleros. He decided to show the place to Jon and store emergency provisions here in barrels. They would be safe, he reckoned, if he left a gift for the Indians. He gathered deadwood and left some phosphorous matches in a tin, against a stormy day. Then he headed down the canyon.

As the spring advanced, Nathaniel worried anew about the security of his little family. One day he and the boy dragged logs and rocks to the stronghold above the ciénaga. He checked the provisions at the cave at the peak, and left a new gift for visitors there. He rode restlessly down to the rincon and out into the Altar Valley, where he studied the wind-blown grasses. He saw nothing.

In April the high tinajas were bone dry, and Nathaniel began the spring gather. He and the boy trapped most of the wily critters at the cave, or at the one remaining seep. But they saw dozens more they couldn't reach, scattered out upon distant ridges and saddles. They collected thirty-seven cows and a dozen calves after exhausting days of hunting, and glumly drove their ravaged herd down to the mesquite corrals.

The glowing iron seared an H into the bellowing calves. A knife cut the young bulls, and then they staggered up one by one, insulted by pain and fear, but full of young life.

"Not much of a gather," said Nathaniel moodily to Patience. "The pumas will get us before the Oliveras will."

She rubbed his shoulders gently after a long day of branding.

"Nathaniel—we could go back to Tucson. You could start a freight line with our mule team and wagon . . ." she said eagerly.

"You aren't very happy here, are you," he said as a statement.

She smiled.

"You're my happiness. Wherever you are, that's where I'm happiest."

He turned to gaze at the slim, erect woman who loved him so unreservedly. Their eyes met, and some ancient fire passed between them.

"But you're lonely."

"Yes. With you and Jonathan gone almost every day I have no one . . . only Charity. I keep busy but it's often so hard and dull. I wish Concepcion were here! Anyone! Anyone!"

Then suddenly there were tears upon her cheeks, a thing that was rare in her. He sat silently, troubled.

"Perhaps you'll soon meet Maria Louisa Olivera," he said softly.

His thought startled her. Often in her mind's eye she had imagined the Olivera phaeton driving up the canyon, with the young Mexican woman coming to call on her new neighbor.

"Oh, Nathaniel!"

"We've got to do something," he sighed. "Even with the calves, we have only half the cattle we started with. The lions got the rest. . . . The pasture I thought would prosper us has only devoured us. I suppose that's why there are no Olivera cattle up there, in spite of the water. The Arizona country turned out to be more than a dumb Yankee farmer like me can handle."

She felt his defeat and hugged him wordlessly.

"I don't think the lions would come down to the rincon," he said. "But putting cattle out there is a terrible risk."

"Nathaniel, I don't think there are even enough cattle to start over with . . . and we don't have much money left. It would take years to build the herd large enough . . ."

She was right.

"I don't know the answer. But we've got to get all the cattle off the mountain and down on the rincon, that's for sure," he muttered. "We're safe enough here, hidden like this. But out there, we'll be found out fast. I was hoping for two or three years . . . time to expand, hire a few hands . . ."

"You could go see them," she suggested. "No one ever does. Everyone's afraid to, and maybe that's their mistake. They never try to be neighborly and come to an agreement first."

"If I went to see them, would you stick it out here awhile more?" he asked.

"I'll do what I must," she replied.

He grinned. "There's never been a man I couldn't come to an agreement with."

He began to feel better. "We'll put our cattle out on the rincon, then. And in a few days I'll saddle up and pay a neighborly visit."

That afternoon the whole family drove the cattle down to the rincon. They rode merrily behind bawling animals, down the twisting canyon trail, and then around the last bend and out upon the rolling desert. The cattle slowly fanned out upon the good grama grass that bunched high amid prickly pear.

Nathaniel reined up beside Patience. "I claimed the rincon," he said softly. "It runs from here south to the border. That leaves the Altar Valley proper to the Oliveras, and everything west of here is ours."

"If," she replied, wryly.

They watched a column of vultures wheel in the haze to the southeast.

"Something died over there," he said uneasily. "Come on, Patience. Jonathan! Charity! It's high time we headed back home!"

CHAPTER 4

The column of Sonoran vultures wheeled lazily through the April morning. Far below, in a sandy arroyo where the mesquite grew thick, there were more of the great redheaded oily blackbirds burdening limbs, along with a cohort of ravens and hawks.

An ancient bronzed shaman walked lightly toward the column, knowing what he would find. All too often, for as long as he could remember, he had found the bodies of his people: women and children as well as warriors and hunters, who came here to the ancient Papago homelands for meat or beans or cactus fruit.

He walked delicately, this desiccated old one who had seen more summers than he could count. He was so light that he left no impression in the sands, no marks of passage.

But he had amazing endurance for one so ancient, and he often walked a day and a night without weariness, finding nourishment among the prickly pear, saguaro, and mesquite.

The sweet foul stench told Night Hawk that he was close, but it was an odor he was familiar with, and he ignored it. He padded down into the arroyo and the great black flock flapped violently into the hot sky. A coyote turned and bounded abruptly away from his meal.

The old Papago recognized all three of the bronzed bodies, even though the wild creatures had dined upon them for a day and the flesh was far gone. The dead man and his two sons lived in Night Hawk's own village. They had been hunting here, and had become the hunted.

Night Hawk stared bitterly at the bullet holes: one in the chest of the man; another through the eye of the older boy. The younger one's head had been bashed in. Their two burros and the mustang had died of slit throats. The burros and the horse were almost white skeletons but the leggings and camisas of the men had slowed the animals.

The holy man stood stock still, his obsidian eyes absorbing every detail until he could reconstruct the whole story. There would be wailing in another hogan soon when he brought the news. He walked over to the dead father and lifted a necklace of turquoise with a medal of St. Christopher over the eyeless head.

There was one more thing to look for: the prints of a shod horse, prints leading back to the Hacienda del Leon far to the east. He found them. He knew the horse—a dun the very color of the desert. And he knew the killer, a thin, pasty-white hombre with a strange bulging forehead and a skull so huge in relation to his jaw that his head resembled a gourd.

The Evil One, he thought. *The Gourd Head,* with the darting eyes and the flaccid posture and the slouch of the spine in the saddle. Even now, Night Hawk supposed, the man would be cleaning la pistola and el fusil in front of his casita near the corrals.

The venerable one rested on his staff—a staff he could thrust with deadly skill, though even his own people didn't know that—and let the spirits whisper in his ears. He listened, and raised his furrowed face to the sacred mountain. He began to walk north toward a canyon where the other white men had built a new casa. It was time to present himself to them.

He knew he would be safe going to the gray-eyed man and blue-eyed woman. With Don Ignacio he would not be safe, for the Oliveras allowed no Papagoes into the Altar Valley. Nor Apaches from the east, nor Yaqui from the south, nor Seri from the land beside the great sea. Patricio, who came first, had decreed death to all Indians who ventured upon his lands, the lands a distant king had taken from Night Hawk's people.

It was a terrible thing, the medicine man reflected. The Altar Valley, at the foot of the sacred mountain, had been the ancestral home of his people, but now they were driven west, almost out of sight of Elder Brother.

The Olivera policy had not been all bad for the Papagoes. It had sometimes prevented the terrible Apaches from sweeping down upon their villages, killing men and stealing burros and women. The Mexicans had rained death upon the Apaches even more than they had tormented the Papagoes.

But that was a blessing his people could do without, Night Hawk thought. It would be better if there were no Mexicans and his bean-eating people had their home back. They slipped into the forbidden valley anyway, because the Olivera forces were spread thin over the vast desert. They came to Baboquivari because they had to: the rites of passage required that the young men come to imbibe the wisdom of Elder Brother. And they came as well to hunt and gather beans, because the Altar Valley was abundant, while the lands of exile were barren.

They came and sometimes they died, the old man thought. Died because Ignacio Olivera employed a manhunter to kill them, a murderer who stalked his people as a hunter stalks the deer.

He crossed the rincon, heading for the mouth of the

canyon that led to the sacred mountain, and found knots of cattle grazing peacefully. He approached one group and it did not bolt away. The cattle never did when he passed. He observed the large fresh H burned rawly into the calves.

A few yards farther the old shaman found the fresh tracks of another shod horse. They were only hours old. The edges were sharp and the wind spirits had not yet dislodged grains of sand and dropped them into the shiny bottom of the hoofprints.

He studied the impression of the shoe and recognized it. The horse had been shod by the farrier at the Hacienda del Leon. The old Indian had seen a thousand other prints like these. But this was not the sign of the Evil One. He knew the dun's stride better than he knew his own face.

He followed the footprints westward. The horse had stopped. Its rider had paused to observe something. The cattle with the H? The prints turned northward, following the cloven hoofmarks of the cattle in the sand.

Night Hawk followed them for an hour, noticing where the horse had paused. And then, near the mouth of the canyon, the rider turned east in a hurry: the prints were those of a running horse.

So, he thought, the settlers in the canyon had been discovered. Soon the Oliveras would come to kill them or drive them away. These newcomers were in mortal danger—a matter of hours.

The ancient shaman paused to consider. Let the whites kill the whites, he thought. The bean-eating people would benefit. But the thought had not been sent by Elder Brother, and the shaman was mortified. He knew that the whites in the canyon were a different nation, and perhaps could be allies of his people. He would warn them. It would be an act of peace at the very toes of the sacred mountain.

Night Hawk slipped silently up the canyon to the Hapgood meadows, a wraith so invisible that no animal fled as he passed. He paused as the sunlit meadow came into view, and once again was amazed at the industry of these people. There was a new adobe shed near the corral, and a ramada of ocotillo poles along the front of the casa.

And there was peace in the meadow, the peace that Night Hawk reciprocated as he slipped quietly to a point only twenty feet from where Nathaniel was scything tall grass.

The slender Yankee, absorbed in the rhythm of the blade, did not see his visitor for some minutes. But when he finally lifted his eyes he discovered a tiny, very erect Indian a few yards away. His heart thudded. He had not been careful. The Winchester was back at the casa.

Still, this was an ancient one. He rested upon his staff. A red kerchief across his forehead, knotted behind, held the man's dusky gray hair in place. Those jet-black eyes stared evenly at Nathaniel, but there was no hostility in them, and Nathaniel slowly relaxed.

He laid the scythe on the ground before him. But he could not help glancing fearfully into the ridges and rocks to see whether the old Papago was alone or one of many.

"*Buenos días,*" said the old one quietly. "*Habla español?*"

"No, I don't rightly do. A few words. But my wife—*mi esposa*—and the muchacho speak it. They picked it up in Tucson."

The old one nodded.

"Peace," he said in English. "Peace, Nay-than-yel, Paychance, Jon-ah-than, Char-tee."

Nathaniel was amazed.

"I watch and listen many moons," the Indian explained. "I am Papago. *Santo hombre. Muy viejo.* You will call me Night Hawk."

Nathaniel sighed, wondering how often and how closely they had been observed in their daily rounds, all the while unsuspecting.

"*Bienvenido, amigo.*" Nathaniel grinned, discovering wry humor in it.

"Pa! Pa! Are you all right?" Jonathan burst from the casa with a Winchester glinting in his hand.

"Jonathan, take it easy," Nathaniel called. "We have a friend here. Now set down that gun."

The youth obeyed reluctantly.

"Translate for me, Jonathan. Welcome him as our honored guest and invite him to share a meal with us."

But the Indian addressed the boy at length.

"He says we're trespassing in the sacred mountains of his people and defiling the hogans of the gods."

"Tell him there was no one here—we claimed it," Nathaniel flared. "No. Wait. Tell him we do not wish to offend his people but only raise cattle peacefully here. Ask him if we can make amends or a peace offering of some kind."

Those obsidian eyes absorbed it all: the first as well as the last. Night Hawk stood silent for a long moment.

"Tell your father I will share your meal," he said at last.

Patience watched curiously while the old one ate in the shade of the ramada. After a while Charity stopped clinging to her mother's skirts and sat down shyly beside the shaman. Night Hawk wasn't much over four feet but there was a palpable dignity and authority about him that was felt by all the Hapgoods.

He stood up in the long light and addressed them.

"Many moons ago," he said, "when the sun was rising behind Baboquivari, I had a great vision. The coyote spirit said to me, white men will come to the sacred mountain. Go and watch them. If they are full of greed and arrogance and take our land from us, they will be enemies. But if they come peacefully and feed and shelter the Papago people, they will be friends and the mountain spirits will guard them. That was the vision of Night Hawk."

He was silent for a long moment.

"We wish to have peace with our neighbors," Nathaniel responded. "As a token of it, I have a gift for you."

He rummaged in the casa and returned with his fine bowie knife in its leather sheath, and placed it in the shaman's hands.

The medicine man drew the blade and found the edge keen. "It will cut the way a leaf cuts the wind," he said quietly.

The sun plunged down behind the western ridge and a chill current of air drifted down the canyon from the peak.

"I have come to warn you that you have been discovered. The Oliveras have seen your cattle, and they will come soon. Maybe tomorrow."

The words chilled Nathaniel.

"But—we moved the cattle out only two days ago!"

"It was an unfortunate time," the shaman said slowly.

"What will happen?" Patience asked fearfully.

The tiny man stared up at her unblinkingly.

"You could die," he said.

The evening air was suddenly cold upon her shoulders.

"If they send the Evil One alone, you will die. If others come, you might live."

"The Evil One?" Nathaniel asked.

"Two days ago the Evil One killed three more of my people," the shaman said. "The Evil One stalks the Papagoes. He has killed more than ten times the fingers on my hands. And now there will be weeping in another hogan.

"You are not safe here. Soon the Evil One will stalk you the way he stalks the Papago. We have a name for him—Head-Like-a-Gourd-Who-Kills."

"Who might he be?" Nathaniel asked thoughtfully.

"You will know him when you see him," the shaman replied. "When he comes, all the world is silent. The birds are silent. The wind dies. The coyote does not bark."

"Why does he kill your people?" Nathaniel asked.

The obsidian eyes glittered in the glow of sunset.

"He is sent by the Oliveras to keep us away from the land they stole from us. They told us we would die if we returned. But we come. We must come to Baboquivari. And sometimes we die. We must always come to the sacred mountain or the Papagoes will disappear from the earth. Not even the Oliveras can take the sacred mountain from us or drive Elder Brother from his home."

His old eyes stared off to the west and his tormented people beyond the ridges.

"One more thing. You have stored barrels in the sacred cave of Elder Brother."

"Yes . . . I hope we haven't—"

"Nothing that is placed on the floor of his cave can remain there for more than a few moons. The time will come when Elder Brother casts it out upon the rocky slope."

Nathaniel was mystified. "You mean your Papago shamans will move the barrels?"

"No. Elder Brother will move them himself," the shaman said sharply, his eyes full of menace. "Now I must go. I must take this"—he held up the St. Christopher medal—"to the hogan where the widow lives. Remember—beware the Evil One."

"Wait! Is there anything we should do—to defend—to prepare?"

The old one stared at Nathaniel.

"You have a strong spirit; stronger than the spirit of the other. Be strong. Be strongest when you are weakest."

He walked wordlessly into the twilight, on down the silent canyon, and then a gust of night air blew sparks from the cookfire into the heavens.

Nathaniel stood, puzzling over the opaque message of the wizened man.

Tomorrow.

He looked painfully at the woman he loved, and the children he loved, wondering if they would soon be sacrificed to his bullheadedness. All the warnings he had heard echoed in his mind.

"I know what's going through your mind, Nathaniel Hapgood, and it's not like you," she scolded. "You used to say that the best lives weren't the safest ones."

"We could still make it. Hitch up the mules; load the freighter—"

"Stop that!" She whirled around to face him. "Yes, we could run. But you'd never be the same. You'd die inside!"

He grinned at her.

"There isn't any other man like you," she said quietly. "I knew that from the day we met. It's the man in you I love. That and the quality called character. . . . Oh, Nathaniel—"

"I thought you wanted to go back and start a freight business. Leastwise that's how I heard you the other day," he mocked.

"I was lonely."

"Are you ready to take on the Oliveras? An army of pistoleros? Do you know what they'd do if they caught you alive and killed me?"

"Yes."

"Are you prepared to shoot and kill if necessary?"

". . . Yes."

"Face wounds, and injury, pain, loss?"

"For you, darling." She didn't smile.

He grinned. "I wouldn't have married any other, Patience Hope!" he roared, and he kissed her well and long, until her heart pounded and her blood ran hot and eager. When he released her, her cheeks were flushed and there was fire in her blue eyes.

He sat down under the ramada and watched Jonathan fork hay to the geldings at the corrals, and then trudge through the dusk to the casa.

Nathaniel enjoyed what they had built. The pens were sturdy. The adobe home was strong and defensible, and had become beautiful with Patience's love added to it. She had planted an olive and some fruit trees, too.

"Jonathan"—the boy halted—"sit here for a minute."

The lean youngster eased himself down.

"You translated for us very well," Nathaniel began quietly. "Trouble's coming, maybe tomorrow."

"I know, Pop."

"You're being drafted and we're going off to war. You've grown a lot the last few months. You're almost a man now."

Nathaniel halted uneasily.

"Of course I'll try to ward off trouble. I'd like a palaver with Olivera, and that's what I aim to do. Only mad dogs go warrin' without some talk first. So don't you get to worrying too much."

"Pa . . . Pa . . . I couldn't shoot someone. I just can't. I can shoot a rabbit or a deer, but, Pa, I couldn't, I couldn't . . ." the boy burst out. It had plainly been haunting him ever since Night Hawk left.

The father sighed. "I didn't think I could either, until

they sent me packing in the First Massachusetts. . . . I didn't think I could until I was shot at. Then I could."

"Pop, I'm scared. I don't want to die. Or you to die. Or Mama . . ."

Nathaniel sat quietly for a long moment.

"Fair enough, Jonathan. I won't ask it. But there's some things you could do that would be almighty handy if trouble comes. Things that could save our bacon, protect your mother and me. Make a lot of noise, for instance, with that repeater of yours. You could shoot a horse or two. . . . You're a dead shot; you could shoot a pistol out of a man's hand. All that's better than killing anyway, even in self-defense."

"I could do that," the boy said eagerly. "And I wouldn't even be scared."

"I'll want you up in the stronghold, covering the meadow and us in the casa. You hightail there fast if you hear horses coming up-canyon. Put your Winchester up there tonight, and a couple hundred cartridges, and bring the old Sharps down here for your mother. And don't be scared up there, son. With that lever action you'll likely have more fire power than half a dozen of those hombres. Just keep low and fire through the little ports we arranged in the logs and rock.

"I'm awful scared."

"Well, that's good. People who aren't scared just get themselves killed. But just remember that there's not going to be any shooting. Your pa's going to talk to Olivera. That'll be the sum of it."

But the muscles of Nathaniel's face grew taut as he contemplated the morrow.

CHAPTER 5

For a week after the whipping and the forced march to Tucson, Nathaniel slept restlessly, at first in acute pain, lying on his belly. And then his body began to mend.

Patience sat beside him the weary days and wiped his face with a damp cloth until his low but persistent fever subsided. She shopped the third afternoon, and found some ready-made shirts for Nathaniel and some bib overalls for Jonathan. She engaged Concepcion to sew a few things for herself and Charity. But the Mexican girl was frightened and her visits were brief.

One evening he arose and sat at the window overlooking the dusty plaza of the old pueblo. An hombre in a dirty camisa and stained pantalones lounged darkly in the moonlight against an adobe wall. Nathaniel stared narrowly at the man with a mind full of suspicions.

He had a way of sorting things out, taking stock, weighing possibilities. It was a trait that had evolved from long hours beside a birch-log fire during the New England winters. So it was natural, as he healed, to begin asking and answering crucial questions. What could a Yankee farmer do against an outfit like that? Was there really an Olivera grant or was it a myth? Would the territorial law help? What about Olivera himself? Was he as bad as his hombres?

It was a puzzle, and there was no solution. They could go back to Concord, of course. Start over. There were good farms near the one he had sold. . . . But it was unthinkable. Arizona sort of got to a person, and the desert cast its net upon a man.

He'd failed. He hadn't counted on the pumas. Still, he knew cattle and had built up a fine ranch from nothing. In another year, using the rincon, they'd have squeaked through. It would be a going thing.

Patience slipped up behind him in the moody dark and rubbed his shoulders as he stared down upon the shrouded plaza.

"Want to go back?" he asked sharply. It took her by surprise.

"To the ranch? Yes." Her answer surprised herself. "But I don't want for you—or us—to be hurt. Not again."

"I'll have to go see him. Everything seems to hinge on that. I'll try some fancy talking. I doubt that the old buzzard is as bad as his crew."

"You could ask him about our cattle," she said.

"I'll do it, then," he said. "We won't know which way to jump until we talk to him."

He turned to face her in the lamplight.

"Patience, are you sure you want to go back? Face the loneliness again? That sweat and cold and heat and hard living and danger?"

"I was lonely . . . but, yes, I do. Tucson's not the same. Even Concepcion seems frightened to be with us. It's as if that man's power extends even to here, and makes us outcasts. It's funny, but I keep remembering the desert after a rain. The greasewood smell. The mesquite fires. You with the horses. My children growing so fast and straight. Yes, Nathaniel, yes!"

That settled it. The next morning he eased out of the

hotel, a little weak on his pins. A lounging Mexican suddenly lifted his head alertly.

"I'm being watched," Nathaniel muttered to himself. "I suppose Olivera wants to know whether I'm going to retaliate. He'll spend a few pesos to keep an eye on me. Well, I'll give him something to think about."

He wheeled into the emporium of Jasper Wiggin and emerged minutes later with a lever-action carbine, and another Colt, this time an army model. His observer was doing a bad job of feigning disinterest. At the saddlery next door he bought a bedroll, canteen, saddlebags, lariat, knife, and slicker. In a musty mercantile across the plaza he provisioned.

There was a temper building up in him. He liked the feel of the Colt slung over his hip and the brass forty-four–forties in the loops of the belt. He was far from through with the Baboquivari ranch.

He glanced at the gaunt shadow skulking ten or twenty paces back. There'll be a new wing on that casa, he thought. Tile floors. A dug well hooked to a windmill. A good wagon road out to the Altar Valley. Some registered Hereford bulls.

He remembered the lashing of the bullwhip, terrible, blinding, unending. And now there would be Olivera vaqueros living in his own house, sleeping in his and Patience's bed, eating from her table. The thought galled him. He whirled to stare at his clumsy shadow with such glinting menace that the hollow-eyed man shrank from his gaze.

He stalked through the hotel and crashed into their rooms and unloaded his mound of purchases with a thump.

Patience laughed. "You're well again," she said, pleased to see life and anger and spirit in her man.

He hugged her long, and left at dawn on the bay, down

the Nogales Road in the valley of the Santa Cruz. Where the Santa Ritas loomed highest to the east, he cut west on the trail to old Arivaca. And after resting at the lake there, beneath noble cottonwoods, he eased down the long westward trail into the Altar Valley and the hacienda of the Oliveras.

Nathaniel pulled up Cotton Mather on a gentle rise a few hundred yards east of the Hacienda del Leon. The rested bay showed no sign of weariness, even after a day and a half of travel.

There was no one in sight. Not a soul. There had been no one on the wagon roads. The oblong casa stood on a delta near the junction of two wide arroyos, in a shallow basin. The building had massive vigas emerging from its roofline, and an atrium at the rear, surrounded by living quarters with a red tile roof. The casa opened on a great square, around which were clustered adobe homes and bunkhouses. Across the south end of the square were adobe sheds that opened onto extensive corrals with stout mesquite walls that would protect cattle and horses from winter winds. The place was a small village, really, although it was one family's ranch. Off to the west, perhaps a quarter of a mile, Nathaniel could see a dam across the great arroyo, and behind it a glistening lake with hundreds of multicolored cattle dotting the shores. To the south somewhere, but not visible, was the border of Mexico. There was no fence.

Nathaniel unbuckled his gunbelt and stowed his Colt in a saddlebag. It would not do to enter the place armed. He touched his heels to the bay and began the soft descent to the casa. As he approached, a stream of people emerged from an adobe building, and their Sunday finery made him realize it was the sabbath.

The candles guttered at the altar of the adobe chapel while the Franciscan padre from San Xavier del Bac said mass. The square chapel had been built by Don Ignacio's grandfather, and now an itinerant priest came once a month to bring the sacrifice of the mass to these souls beyond the parishes of the Church. Don Ignacio sat contentedly, and thanked the *buen Dios* for his good fortunes. Maria, handsome in a white linen dress and an exquisite black lace mantilla over her head, sat beside him. And next to her was the attentive Capitán Castillo-Armas, who had brought good news to the hacienda.

They had encountered some sharp resistance from the Norte Americanos and had taken them to Tucson. No one was hurt. The Hapgoods left behind a small casa with good corrals and a good water supply that would serve the hacienda well. And he had charged the Hapgoods the half of their cattle and their possessions for trespassing and pasturage. The capitán had brought back a family Bible that he regretted keeping, but there had been no other difficulty.

Don Ignacio did not pity the evicted strangers. They were not Mexicans and they were on land controlled by the hacienda. Their calamities were no doubt the will of an angry God. And the object lesson would not be lost upon the land-hungry rabble of Tucson.

Mass was compulsory at the hacienda. The Oliveras had always looked after the spiritual well-being of their vaqueros and their families. There were close to sixty people crowded into the chapel, hearing the words of life from the good padre. Don Ignacio took pleasure at this gathering of the hacienda, and its traditions.

Behind him somewhere was Talliferro, communing with God. Ignacio smiled sardonically at the thought. God would have a great struggle rescuing the soul of that wretch who never went to confession. He sighed uneasily.

Talliferro was essential. The patrón believed the man had murdered perhaps twenty Papagoes, God rest their souls. But the terror had kept peace on the western flank of the hacienda. Life was hard in the wilderness, and Ignacio never doubted that God understood certain difficulties. Still . . . it would be best if he were to undertake a certain penance.

It was the custom for the patrón to leave first, and now Don Ignacio, Maria, and the capitán knelt briefly before the altar and emerged into a blinding sun.

The capitán saw Nathaniel first, and nudged Ignacio.

"Look, it's the insolent Hapgood," he snapped.

But the patrón smiled and strode toward the gringo as he dismounted. Nathaniel found himself facing the short leonine patrón, whose face was a cordial mask. And beside Olivera was the one Nathaniel hated, the one whose whip he still felt through his whole body.

"You will please come in, Señor Hapgood. Juanita, some cool water from the olla. Pepito, take this caballo to the corrals and feed it. You will stay for dinner, sir."

The capitán nodded curtly and excused himself.

Nathaniel was ushered into a long room with a great fireplace at one end and exposed vigas above. Massive furniture stood starkly against whitewashed walls. The Spanish genius of bringing austerity and luxury to the same place was evident here.

"Let us get to your business at once," said Ignacio. "You are the Norte Americano who brought cattle to Baboquivari and built a rancho on our lands."

"Yes. My wife, Patience, and I did build a ranch on land we believed to be unclaimed and west of your grant . . ." he began.

"And now you want your cattle back, yes? Perhaps it can be arranged," said Ignacio. "I have a family Bible of yours here, and I wish to return it with apologies. That you were not permitted to take it was most regrettable. . . ."

"Señor Olivera—I thank you for the Bible. But—you see —we wish to return to our land. We filed a claim on it. There's no record of your grant or deed in Tucson or Prescott. It's common knowledge that your family holds a Spanish crown grant on the Altar Valley, but surely you realize that most of my claim is west of you—"

"I see, Mr. Hapgood. Most regrettable, this confusion. You were on our land. My family's controlled these mountains for a century. The Gadsden Purchase changed nothing. The ownership of property is in your Constitution, is it not?"

Olivera was not in a mood to argue and wished to halt this unpleasant intrusion upon a sleepy Sunday as fast as possible.

"Señor Olivera, what *is* your boundary? We couldn't find a record anywhere," Nathaniel responded.

"We've never recorded it with your officials. Never will. One copy is here; the other's in Spain. . . . The grant is parchment. The reality is that we defend what is ours with whatever force is necessary. That's the reality, Mr. Hapgood."

"Well, I'm trying to settle this reasonably, and I've come a long way to do it," Nathaniel persisted. "I want my ranch back. I want to know a few simple facts. Where's your line? At the foothills? At the ridges? On a meridian? Let's get it straightened out while I'm here!"

"Ah, Mr. Hapgood. I'll tell you a secret. Our grant says only that the Oliveras shall possess the Altar Valley from the thirty-first parallel to the thirty-second, and from foothills to foothills. We've always defined that in the broadest way. My father and grandfather before me. And we've spilled blood for it. Let me be precise. Forget that place, Mr. Hapgood. It doesn't belong to you."

Nathaniel tried a new tack.

"Señor, you're surely aware that—well, look. Some of the lowland we claimed is probably yours. We'll get off. Or we could buy it and pay with either cattle or gold. I think we can come to an agreement that would benefit us both."

"No," Ignacio snapped.

"Well, now, there's some question of who's trespassing against whom. You're on my property," Nathaniel said hotly.

"No, no, no, Mr. Hapgood. Let us talk of more pleasant things."

"I intend to return to my home."

"It will be at your mortal peril."

"I'll risk it! I'll keep off the rincon until a court settles whose it is. But we're going home, and any Olivera hombre on my place is going to get himself a trip to the sheriff and a complaint."

The patrón eyed his adversary levelly, assessing the man. Nathaniel stood a foot taller, but the compact patrón radiated power and will, so that he seemed somehow larger and more dangerous.

"As you wish," he said at last.

But Nathaniel was seething. "You've a valley a hundred miles long and fifteen wide. Isn't that enough?"

Don Ignacio turned into a pillar of ice. "Mr. Hapgood, dinner will be served in a moment. You will wish to freshen yourself, and then I shall inquire about your civilization on your east coast. Here, Juanita, show the señor the way. . . . Mr. Hapgood, let us break bread together. My daughter, Maria, and I will have one other guest, Capitán Pedro Castillo-Armas, whom you have met."

The meal went badly despite Ignacio's efforts to bring pleasantry to his table. Nathaniel withdrew into himself. His tormentor sat opposite in silent disapproval. Maria sensed animosity and ate quietly, understanding little of the English.

Ignacio made desultory conversation. He had broad interests and would have liked to plumb Nathaniel's knowledge of the government in Washington, ranching, mining, and especially the ferrocarriles that were being laid at breakneck speed across the continent.

But Nathaniel, no master of persiflage, was feeling the weight of defeat and frustration.

"Come, I will show you the hacienda," said the patrón, setting aside his napkin. "And then you will wish to return to Tucson—where your family is safe."

The compact man led the taller one to the adobe chapel.

"My grandfather built it before he built the casa," Don Ignacio said. "He dedicated it to Mexico's beloved Virgen de Guadalupe, who is also patroness of our hacienda."

To one side there was a niche with an image of the virgin, exquisitely painted, surrounded by gold leaf and roses.

"My wife, Luz, God rest her soul, brocaded the altar cloth and these vestments. Exquisite. To the glory of God, yes?"

Children rollicked in the plaza, and Nathaniel noticed that the adobe casitas around its perimeter formed a natural fortress. There was a large dug well near the corrals, from which youths were bucketing water to horses. A dozen high-walled pens of mesquite stretched southward toward a great arroyo. Some had a few horses in them, and one had dairy cows.

"These horses have Andalusian and Spanish Barb blood," Ignacio said proudly. "For generations, we have crossed them with the best mustangs, horses that came from the conquistadors. They have the beauty of Arabians, and endurance to live on this desert. My grandfather started them, importing white stallions from Spain. Some of these pigs, the vaqueros, are hard on them, but these horses survive even my vaqueros," he said grimly. "I box their ears but it is no use."

They walked quietly up a broad, sandy arroyo to the west, the ranch's aorta. They came to a rocky narrows where there was a well-wrought masonry dam rising twenty feet and stretching a hundred.

"It took ten stonemasons from Hermosillo half a year to build it," he said. "A masterpiece, yes?"

A rare smile lit Ignacio's face.

"This was my own project, and it has allowed us to double the cattle in this area, and even irrigate a few hectares. It forms a lake a quarter mile long. It was half a mile ten years ago, but the arroyo carries tons of sand when it runs, and now my lake decreases every year. Someday—perhaps after I'm gone—there will be only sand," he sighed. "But now, it is magnificent, yes?"

It was indeed. The spot had a lovely aspect, and Ignacio had built a level patio to one side of the dam, with terraced gardens and some furniture where people could take their leisure in the sun or shade. Near the patio was a small niche with a finely wrought figure of the Virgen de Guadalupe.

"She is here to protect and bless this water," Ignacio said, eying the sectarian at his side.

They brought Nathaniel's saddled mount to him and he left in the late afternoon, riding north in the twilight. He made a dry camp and awoke before dawn, feeling drained. The events of the last several days had taken a toll. The whip wounds had healed, but travel, discouragement, and sheer fatigue all caught up with him that morning.

There was a slice of dull light along the northeast horizon, so he rose. Cotton Mather would need water soon.

The going would be cooler now than later. So he shook out his boots for scorpions and broke camp, feeling the need for a week of sleep.

A ghostly light began to glow off the sheer eastern face of Baboquivari, so that the peak was disembodied from its black base, and glowed in the murky northern sky. Then the long rays of the early sun turned the peak into a tower of flame against the hushed blue of the west. The home of Indian spirits was visible for a hundred miles. Nathaniel remembered that at the very foot of that glowing peak, still shrouded in night, was a cave where he had stored water, food, ammunition, and supplies.

He turned the gelding toward the mountain rather than Tucson. He would reconnoiter a bit. See who lived in his house, and where his cattle were.

He rode toward a ridge that he knew would lead him to a thicket of juniper overlooking his home in the canyon. Once before he had been there and had watched Patience rub their clothing on a washboard and hang it to dry in the desert sun.

There was a thin line of smoke from the kitchen chimney, and four strange horses in the corral. The garden had been watered. His eight mules were in the pasture. Several of his cattle stood at the ciénaga. Nathaniel crouched on the ridge until his knees ached, but he saw no one. Some hombres were there, but he didn't know how many. It was important to know.

Cotton grew restless, and there was mounting danger that he would smell one of the horses below and whinny, so Nathaniel reluctantly eased back from the ridge and reined the bay toward the peak, and then around the shoulder to the west, and the fallen slab of rock, and the cave. He unsaddled the horse and shooed him toward the pool while his eyes adjusted to the gloom. And then he saw a man.

Night Hawk's white hair was all he saw at first, but it was enough to keep him from clawing at his Colt. The old shaman stood calmly while Nathaniel absorbed his presence, and then said, *"Bienvenido."*

Nathaniel relaxed. The old man unrolled a pack with tortillas and frijoles and silently thrust them at Nathaniel, who ate gratefully.

"Dos vaqueros en casa," Night Hawk said. With stick drawings, a few English words, and some Spanish, the old Indian explained that the vaqueros had done nothing but move in. Hapgood's cattle were all there. Nothing had been taken.

Then the shaman turned silent for a long moment, and somehow conveyed the urgency of what he was about to say. He had had a vision that very dawn. The spirits had come to him. Baboquivari had turned blood red. The coyote spirit had said, Tell the white man not to return with his family now. There was danger. Later, the spirits who lived on the sacred mountain would make it safe. But not just yet.

The old man's jet-black eyes bored into Nathaniel's.

The Yankee sighed, and thanked the shaman. The Papago, too, had a claim—the best claim—to these mountains. Perhaps the old medicine man knew that the longer he kept the white men away, the less likely it would be that they'd return.

Nathaniel was weary, and the old man's visions didn't seem very important.

"I warned Olivera we'd be coming," he grunted. "I can't rightly back down now."

The Indian nodded. They sat quietly an hour, watching the sun sink, and then Night Hawk slipped out into the night, and didn't return.

CHAPTER 6

Nathaniel fell into a drugged sleep and didn't awake until nearly noon. He felt better. His mind was clear. He woke up knowing exactly what he would do.

He reckoned that his first step was to spirit his cattle to some hiding place where the Oliveras couldn't get at them. He'd have to look for a canyon off to the west, on Papago land, with water. He and Jonathan would have to move them over there a few at a time right in front of the noses of those vaqueros, but they would have to move fast before the Oliveras rounded up the herd.

His second task was to recover his freight wagon, mules, and household goods, and the lever-action rifles. He could earn a living with that wagon and team. But getting his goods away from those vaqueros at the casa would be no mean trick. It took an hour even to harness the mules and hook them to the wagon tongue.

The next steps would be tougher, and he had no ready answer to the questions they raised. First they had to drive off the Olivera hombres, and then reclaim their ranch. That boded some sort of gunfight if the men resisted. He dreaded the thought: one New England farmer against excellent Mexican pistoleros. And there was no assurance they could hang on to their ranch once they got it back. He had two warnings: Olivera told him

to stay away, and Night Hawk told him not to return just
now. He sighed, unhappily, not knowing what to do.

There was no way to resolve the matter now. His im-
mediate business was to rescue his cattle and possessions.
With these, he had some leverage and wealth.

All of this flooded through his mind as he brewed cowboy coffee in an old can over a tiny fire of pine twigs. Irritably, he brushed the burrs from Cotton Mather and
pulled a cholla thorn from a fetlock. Then he threw on
the blanket and saddle, and drew up the latigo. He
sniffed the scented air. There was some dampness in it.
Some puffball clouds were drifting from the southeast,
and one was snagged on the peak above.

He decided he'd spend a couple of days here studying
the land to the west for a place to hide his cattle. Damned
if he'd just quit! He gazed down on layer after layer of
blue ridges, some of which radiated out from the sacred
mountain, while others lay crosswise, with no rhyme or
reason to their slopes. Off on the horizon was the brown
flatland where the Papagoes had been driven. But off to
the northwest was a peculiar purplish vee that promised
grass and water. He decided to go there.

He checked his new Colt, which used the same cartridges as the Winchester. The new carbine had a saddle
ring, which allowed him to loop a thong over the saddle
horn so that the carbine hung vertically, barrel down,
easy to grab. He was no hand with a gun, but had taught
himself to go slow, rest the barrel on anything handy, and
squeeze gently.

He noticed that Cotton was missing a shoe on a hind
foot and that the hoof walls had been torn by the
clinched nails. That was serious business. In this sort of
rock, Cotton's hoof would wear to the quick and start
hurting in no time. There were shoes and nails at the casa
—where he couldn't go.

He picked up the rear hoof. There was plenty of growth there; the torn walls weren't as serious as they looked. But for now, he'd have to devise a remedy, and fast.

There was some rawhide in one barrel. He stretched it out and cut an oval piece with his knife, and notched the perimeter. He soaked the rawhide in the pool until it was sopping clear through, and then he set Cotton's foot on it and pulled the flaps up around the hoof. Then he laced thong through the flaps until the boot was secure. When the rawhide dried it would shrink into an iron-hard boot. He cut some spare boots while he waited for the one on Cotton to dry in the hot sun, and tucked them in his saddlebag.

When the boot was dry Nathaniel headed west, down a plunging slope. Cotton slid through loose rubble, sometimes on his rump, until they reached a high plateau that formed the crest of a long ridge. He could see the vee off to the north, but this high table route seemed the best way there.

He worked west for three miles, losing altitude all the while. He found no way to break north. That country was a jumble of canyons, sheer walls, barrancas, and cactus forests. So he kept the gelding on a westward line down a ridge to nowhere.

Eventually the ridge narrowed to a razor top, jumbled with rocky fingers, and came to an abrupt halt at a headland. He found a trail dropping off to the north and took it. At the bottom he would have to work around the headland and up toward the great canyon he had seen.

The trail took him into a valley with a grove of sycamores. The trail here was wide and well traveled, and he thought he saw the vague imprint of a moccasined foot, as well as some unshod pony prints in dried mud. A little lower he spotted a turkey vulture feather pinioned beneath a small rock pointing toward the sacred peak. He was on a Papago trail. He watched the bay's ears and eyes, and wherever the horse looked, so did Nathaniel. He unhooked the thong over the Colt's hammer, just in case.

The trail turned west, so he abandoned it and struggled through almost impassable country full of dead ends and arroyos. He was forced to backtrack frequently, but after an hour he could see what was probably the mouth of the great canyon. He was traveling crosswise of the drainage from the mountains, so it took three miles of wandering to move one mile north. And every arroyo and ridge became a natural obstacle.

At last he descended a long oak-dotted slope and found himself staring into a majestic canyon, perhaps half a mile across at the top, and two hundred yards wide at the base. The flanks of the eastbound canyon were illumined dazzlingly by the late gold sun of that June evening.

The walls were not sheer, but catapulted up about two thousand feet, and there was dark timber on their upper reaches. The floor was a grassy meadow, sloping toward a wide arroyo that ran along the northern wall. He could see wide parks ahead, and some narrows where rocky fingers reached out into the great canyon itself.

He urged the weary, thirsty bay forward, and soon noticed sheep sign in the grass. Good! There would be a Mexican or Indian here, and water, he thought.

Behind a rock spur he spotted a cabin, and beside it a mass of white sheep. The slanting gold light lit the flanks of the woolly animals as they grazed, and warmed the rust-colored stone that had been carefully laid up with adobe mortar into a finely wrought building. It had a wooden roof with hand-split shakes. Behind it was a sheepfold made of logs dragged down from above, and off to one side, hard against the cliff, was the vivid green

growth that bespoke a spring. In the hollow of rock behind the cabin there was some sort of altar with a heavy
carved crucifix upon it.

A man emerged, wearing the brown cassock of the
Franciscans. He was partly bald and had an aquiline nose
beneath fine brown eyes.

"Bon soir," he said quietly. *"Parlez-vous français?"*

Nathaniel regretted that he did not.

"It doesn't matter," said the man slowly. "I am Pierre
Longet, a brother of the Franciscans. Come water your
horse and join me for a bit of dinner. I have just been
heating some stew. *Votre nom, monsieur?"*

"Nathaniel Hapgood. I guess we're neighbors of sorts.
Your invitation is one I'll just accept with pleasure!" He
was suddenly grateful, and profoundly curious.

"You will wish to freshen yourself and care for your
handsome horse. And then we shall talk," said the monk.

Nathaniel splashed cool spring water over his face
while the bay drank in great gulps. He unsaddled the
gelding and rubbed him down, working up the matted
hair beneath the saddle blanket. The bay found a dusty
basin and rolled happily.

"I believe you have a wife named Patience, a little
daughter named Charity, and a fine son named Jonathan," the Franciscan said with a smile.

Nathaniel was startled. "Why, yes, but how—"

"We'll get to that in time. I'm glad you came. I've been
wishing you would because I've certain things to discuss.
But after dinner. Let me show you my little home. It is an
exquisite locale, *oui?"*

The Franciscan ushered him into an immaculate room,
with whitewashed stone walls. There was a flagstone
floor, polished by use and brooming. Two small windows,
with real glass in them, opened out on the mountains and
down the canyon. There was a simple straw pallet be-

neath a cross, and a pine table and chairs. It was austere and serene.

"Let's sample my mutton, and the legumes from the little garden," he said, ladling the fragrant concoction from the pot. The Frenchman had seasoned the stew magically, and Nathaniel devoured two bowls.

The man was perhaps fifty, Nathaniel thought. He had close-cropped gray hair over his ears, and a fine aristocratic jaw.

"I am actually posted to San Xavier del Bac," the monk began. "I'm a hermit by nature, and so I obtained special permission to come here alone as a mission to the Papagoes. Some of them, you know, live around the mission church near Tucson, but there are many out here who have never been reached. I enjoy my labors here, in this eden, and have brought several souls to the Lord."

"But aren't you in some danger here?"

"Oh, perhaps," replied the monk. "I have no arms, but I'm safe, nonetheless. I have a Protector. And the Papago people are friends. They regard me as a sort of shaman, one of their holy men."

"Like Night Hawk. He must be the one who told you about me and my family."

"Exactly." Brother Pierre smiled. "Night Hawk always stops here going to and from the sacred mountain. He tells me about his tribal spirits, and I teach him the gospels."

The monk's eyes glittered with amusement at the thought of past confrontations.

"He's made no progress with me, and I've made only a soupçon of headway with him! But we've become firm friends, and we share a certain grief about things that befall his people. . . . Tell me about yourself, Monsieur Hapgood."

"We're from New England, near Boston," Nathaniel

began. "I was a farmer. We had a dairy herd, grew hay and a few crops. We came here when the doctors said Patience had consumption. She never really did, but we ended up staying. Desert kind of grew on us."

"Has your family been long in the New World?"

"Yes, the Hapgoods came in the great Puritan migration to Massachusetts Bay Colony in the 1630s. Patience's family came soon after."

"Ah, the Puritans! An austere people, monsieur, but with their eye upon God. Some of my family—in the Loire Valley—became Huguenots in the seventeenth century. I have many cousins who are not Catholic."

"It's an inheritance," Nathaniel sighed.

"Tell me, monsieur, what brings you to this remote place?"

"That's quite a story," Nathaniel said. "I'd guess that Night Hawk has told you much of it."

"He has, but I'd like to hear it from you. Things get lost in the translation."

"We settled last fall in a canyon south of Baboquivari, and ranged our cattle in the mountains," Nathaniel began. "But the lions forced us to graze them down on the rincon off the Altar Valley."

"Which the Oliveras claim."

"Yes. We filed on it, but our right to it is pretty cloudy. At any rate, they found us out a few weeks ago and drove us right off with four armed hombres. It was a hard thing. We left with only the clothing on our backs."

"The Oliveras are hard men," Brother Pierre said slowly.

"Almost everything we own—which isn't much—is still there. And our house is occupied by two of their vaqueros. Our cattle are scattered everywhere. They said they'd round them up and keep half."

"You're lucky," the monk said. "The Oliveras not only

confiscate the possessions of my Papago friends, but their lives as well."

"I rode to the hacienda to have a little palaver with Olivera, but it was like banging on a wall."

There was a silence.

"A priest from our mission attends the Oliveras once a month," said Brother Pierre, breaking the silence. "I have a difficult time teaching the gospel to my flock when the Oliveras keep killing them off."

There was a darkness in his eyes.

"They have a terrible man, pale-skinned, with a huge forehead, who murders my Indians. Night Hawk has seen him; I haven't. I've wondered how much Don Ignacio knows, or how responsible he is, for this—this—"

"A good deal, I suppose," ventured Nathaniel.

"You're probably right," the monk sighed. "The Indians come and accuse me. Ignacio's God is your God, and the patrón sends men to kill us and keep us from our sacred mountain. How do I answer that? I don't," the brother muttered. "It is this man I wish to talk to you about. And these murders."

"I've seen him," Nathaniel said. "Made me squirm."

"I make a little progress, thank God. I have the assistance of Our Lady. We are followers of Francis of Assisi. The Papago know I'm poor and know I love my sheep. And I have found a way to teach them quite a bit."

Nathaniel looked at him quizzically.

"Saint Paul showed me how. He found an altar to the Unknown God in Athens, and boldly proclaimed the Unknown God to the Athenians. The pagans had an inkling of Truth, you see, and Paul made use of it. That's what I do here. I've declared the Great Spirit to them. The Unknown God."

Darkness had come as the sun crept up the canyon

walls until only the highest peaks glowed. They watched the embers of the cookfire in the twilight.

"I'm glad you're here, Father Pierre," Nathaniel said.

"No, no, not a priest. I'm a simple monk. . . . But you've come to this country for a purpose, and you've not told me what it is."

"Yes, I have. I'm looking for a safe place to pasture my cattle for a while, safe from the Oliveras."

"How many are there?"

"Not many. A few dozen are all that are left. Maybe sixty."

"There's grass enough, Monsieur Hapgood. At least for the while. The Lord brought us generous rains last winter, and soon the summer storms will come."

"Then it would be possible?"

"More than possible. This valley shall be a haven for your family as well."

"I can't pay just now for any grass . . ."

"The grass belongs to God, monsieur. Pay him. Perhaps he shall want you to stop this slaughter of my Indians."

Nathaniel stood up, thoughtfully.

"And now, monsieur, you will excuse me while I attend to my devotions. My place is yours. I have some boys, some young catechumens, who could help you with the cattle as well. All that I have is yours."

"I'm grateful," the New Englander said. He unrolled his blanket under a sycamore tree, beneath the Milky Way, with the quiet cropping of the sheep around him in his ears, and slept sweetly.

CHAPTER 7

Patience didn't expect Nathaniel back soon. She worried when he rode away to see Ignacio Olivera. The powerful Mexican was a law unto himself. There were dangers en route. It was a common thing for a man to ride into the wilderness and never be seen again. They died along unknown trails—victims of rattlesnakes, bad water, bucking horses, Indians, sickness, thirst, robbers, cave-ins, and storms.

Her fears continued to gnaw at her in the hot, airless room of the adobe hotel. She was restless in Tucson, and the children were too. She bought two McGuffey's *Readers* and tried some schoolmarming. But Jonathan squirmed and Charity dozed in the hot room. They bolted for the plaza, with its strange people and excitement, whenever Patience let them go. Alone in the room she paced unhappily.

If only she could do something! She hated for all the burden to be on Nathaniel's shoulders. There was nothing to do here, not even cooking. They took their meals in the dining room, and once in a while at a nearby cantina that had fiery food that she ate gingerly and washed down with thick, aromatic coffee.

Their dilemma angered her. They had lost everything. Where was the law? Why couldn't they get help? There

were troops at Fort Lowell, but they were a garrison, and
the bulk of them were tied up by the Apaches. There was
a territorial clerk, but all he would say was that no Olivera grant had been recorded there. Tucson was still a
Mexican town, but boiling with the riffraff of the frontier.

She visited a lawyer one day. Señor Ramon Valenzuela
smiled and told her in heavy accents that not only did the
Oliveras hold a valid royal grant, but had squatter's rights
under the common law of the Norte Americanos. But, he
added, perhaps she could find relief in Prescott, the territorial capital, where the governor and legislature might
be of service. She thanked the attorney and walked back
to the Santa Rita, intrigued with the idea.

She decided to go. It would get the children off the
streets. She could probably return before Nathaniel did.
She turned toward the Butterfield Stage office, west of the
plaza.

"Stage goes twice a week," the skeletal clerk said.
"Leaves at midnight tonight, in fact. That Salt River
country is just an inferno by midmorning and they have
to get past it or kill the horses. That's a danged hard hour
to be leavin' but this time of year it's necessary. Once
they get to the Verde and start climbin' toward the Mo-
gollon Rim, she gets a little cooler. But we'll get you there
ten in the evenin' day after next."

She bought three tickets, packed their few new
clothes in a carpetbag, and wrote a note to Nathaniel telling him where she was going. She entrusted it to the hotel
clerk, and as an afterthought wrote a duplicate and left it
on the washstand beside the china water pitcher. She
didn't know who she'd see in Prescott, but she was eager
to try.

The maroon enamel of the stage glinted darkly in the
glow of the hurricane lamps as Patience and Charity
climbed into the rocking interior. Jonathan wangled a

seat between the burly driver and a gimpy hard-eyed
man with a double-barreled shotgun. There was only one
other passenger, a fat man with muttonchops who eyed
Patience a moment too long and then settled down for an
uncomfortable snooze.

Promptly at midnight the barrel-chested driver yelled
"Har, har, eehar," and cracked his long whistling whip,
and the coach plunged past darkened windows and then
out into the moon-swept desert night.

At five the sun rose and it was instantly hot. It grew fe-
rocious as they rumbled down the grade to the Salt River
and splashed across while the team strained to keep from
miring. By nightfall they were at the Verde River and
heading north up the valley.

In the summer twilight of the following day they rumbled down the piñon-pine hills east of Prescott and into
the rocky basin where the town huddled. The pine-
scented air of the mile-high capital refreshed them after
the ordeal of the desert.

They slept late, with the mountain air in their nostrils
all night. Then the children wanted to explore, so Patience put Charity in the charge of her older brother,
gave him a quarter to squander, and instructed him to report back to the big log hotel frequently. They bolted out
the door.

Patience closed it softly behind them and stretched luxuriously. She intended to take her time. She bathed and
washed her hair while the hotel pressed her gray silk
dress—her only good dress. She whiled away a luxurious
hour, and as a final touch fastened a cameo on a black-
velvet choker to her throat, over the snowy linen of her
blouse. The image in the looking glass smiled back at her,
radiating good health from a fine oval face set in a cas-
cade of glossy brown hair, with just a glint of red in the
sun.

She walked in the cool sun to the fieldstone building that served as the temporary seat of government for Arizona Territory. She had resolved to see the governor himself—what point was there in seeing anyone with less power?

She was ushered in at once and found the man, late a Union cavalry major, immediately accessible. Jameson Canfield, Jr., was an appointee of President Grant and had an eye for such beauty as he now beheld standing before him. Patience flushed at his attentive gaze, and plunged at once into her business, which she described in such spare language and clarity that Canfield's admiring glances settled into respect for a keenly honed mind.

At one point he interrupted.

"Mr. Mendoza, please bring us the army maps of the Altar Valley, the Baboquivari Mountains, and the border west of Nogales. These aren't very accurate, Mrs. Hapgood—lots of terra incognita out there—but they will help."

Mendoza, who clerked at a roll-top desk just outside the governor's chambers, had been listening carefully—that was what Ignacio Olivera paid him a few reales to do each month. He moved swiftly to find the maps and get back to his swiveling stool where even murmured conversations reached his ears.

"Mr. Mendoza, two more requests. As fast as possible, see if there's any copy of the Olivera grant in the office of the registrar of deeds, and see whether the Olivera holdings have been enrolled in the tax records."

Mendoza cursed silently: this would take him away from his listening post for some while. But he raced to locate the information desired by *el gobernador*. He'd have to write Don Ignacio at once. There might even be some extra reales in it!

"I'm glad you came, Mrs. Hapgood." Canfield smiled,

looking into Patience's troubled eyes. "We seem to have something of a Mexican enclave in the territory, quite beyond the reach of our law. I've been aware of the Olivera grant, but never considered it a problem. Now you've brought it into focus for us."

"Major, my husband and I need protection. Can't the Army help us?"

Canfield was amused. "There are four companies, all under strength, in all the territory. A handful are manning the forts—about twenty at Fort Lowell, and half of those on the sick list. The rest are out chasing the Chiricahua Apaches up and down the eastern mountains. As you know, Congress cut the Army to the bone after the war."

"Even if we won our case in the territorial courts we couldn't enforce it," said Patience bitterly. "Ignacio Olivera has an army of pistoleros."

The governor paused, and then chose his words carefully.

"Depends on how much sand you have," he said. "A man can still get settled out here if he's got sand. Gun law's all there is. I'm not approving of it. Just stating the fact. No one ever talks about all the pilgrims who turn tail and go home. The East is full of 'em. You can't blame most of them, either. If the Apaches scalped your husband, what would you do? Stick at the ranch?

"But some hang on out here and prosper, and fight off trouble. I can't rightly say how they do it. Their women are sometimes tougher than the men, and their skinny-legged kids would as soon put a bullet through your hat as look at you. I call it sand, but all those books at West Point call it audacity. You hit 'em where they least expect it, just when they think they've got you running. . . . I can usually tell if a man's got sand just by looking at him."

He unrolled the maps across the conference table.

"Now show me what Olivera claims, and exactly where you are and what you claim."

"It's not what he claims, but what he does with his private army to people like us," she said.

He liked that. She had a way of getting down to the bone.

"Well, maybe the legislature can smoke him out. I can think of a few bills that might do it. Trouble is, they don't meet until January. Half a year from now."

"That's too long," she said.

"Of course the Gadsden Purchase agreement recognized existing private property," he said. "It gave them four years to record their deeds with us. But Mr. Mendoza doesn't seem to be coming up with anything. It makes a man wonder."

She liked the major. His mind was chewing at the problem the way hers did.

Mendoza walked in and reported there were no records —none. His eyes rested on Patience and she felt his gaze before he turned back to his swivel stool.

"He's got all the Altar Valley—looks like it runs well down into Sonora—and your place is where, here?"

"Yes. In the canyon. Nathaniel filed on the mountains, and that rincon, too, this part that's west of the rest of the Altar Valley."

"I'm afraid that's Olivera's if he can rightfully claim the whole valley."

"I suppose so," she sighed. "My husband thinks so, too, but he says there's graze enough to the west for us, if we can control the lions."

"Have you gone to court?"

"No. We'd have to come clear up here—and—what good are claims? We could have an absolute legal right and end up just as dead!" she said hotly.

"That's what concerns me as governor. Is any of that border fenced?"

"No."

"So he's got a large chunk of our territory essentially under Mexican rule. That's something I may have to take up with the State Department. None of our peace officers have ever been on the place. I'd sure like to tie the Stars and Stripes to his flagpole!"

He sat back and mulled the matter for a minute, until Patience thought she'd been forgotten. Then he sat up abruptly.

"I can try a thing or two. Not sure it'll do much good. I'm going to write him immediately. I'll tell him you're going to return to your holding under the protection of the territorial government. I'll warn him that I'll hold him responsible for any harm done to you or your property. And I'll tell him that if he has a valid claim to the country you've settled, he should prove it peacefully in the courts. He'll get a fair hearing. How does that sound?"

"It's more than I hoped." She smiled.

"I've been thinking. I don't believe that old coot wants to be an American citizen. He probably got caught by the Gadsden Purchase. He's a Mexican, and never figured how to handle the new situation except to drive everyone as far away as possible."

She listened, intrigued.

"I've got to squeeze him until he comes in or gets out. Folds up that army of his and joins us, or beats it south."

Her eye caught Mendoza staring through the door.

"The trouble is, I don't have enough lawmen or soldiers in all Arizona Territory to do anything just now. We don't even have our counties organized. I could maybe send a federal marshal down there . . ."

He rose.

She thanked him and emerged into the cool sun, liking

him, liking Prescott, liking civilization and a life more gracious than she had known recently. A part of her wanted to stay, but she knew she had to return to her man, her man who had sand.

The next day they caught the stage to Tucson. And locked in the mail pouch of that very coach was a lengthy letter from the governor to Olivera, and another from Mendoza to Olivera, at an Arivaca address.

Nathaniel was alarmed. Both hotel rooms were empty and anonymous, except that his two new ready-made shirts and some new boots the cobbler had started before he left were in the closet.

He grew irritable. A man likes to come home to his wife, to her softness and smiles. A man likes to share some hours with his youngsters, and guide them in right directions. For a moment he had the feeling he was a bachelor, one of those anonymous men who went to an anonymous place like this each night, to their silent meals. He wanted Patience, and right fast, safe and warm.

Strange how Patience had changed out here, he thought. What had been grave and formal and tender between them had become a rapture, and—he thrust the vision from his mind and stalked the room restlessly. They were probably out eating. Then he spotted the note on the washstand, read it, and worked himself into a temper.

What did she do that for! All that long, hot, dangerous trip for nothing. She wouldn't be back until God knows when. He'd have to eat alone. Running off like that, half-cocked. He sat down in the rocker and rocked it violently until he went over backward with a clatter. He sprawled on the floor and thought he had nearly broken his neck. Suddenly he laughed, and then sighed.

Patience had never done anything very foolish. Perhaps

she was on to something. Maybe she could get the beans out of the pot after all. He admired her then. She had more wisdom behind those grave eyes than he ever reckoned she did.

He walked down to the hotel clerk and asked him to bucket hot water up to the tin bathtub down the hall. The clerk handed him the duplicate letter. He scrubbed the trail grime off, and relaxed in luxury. Dinner at the cantina, some hot enchiladas and things Patience never cooked, and then maybe he'd mosey over to the Butterfield office and find when the next stage from the north was due.

Some enchiladas smothered in a fiery sauce and some frijoles plus a mug of cerveza built a fine volcano in Nathaniel's belly, and he sat back contentedly watching the wide Mexican girl who had served him. There was only one other customer, a cadaverous sad-eyed young hombre in a sweat-stained camisa. The man glanced away.

Nathaniel ambled toward the plaza. The old pueblo came alive in the long June evening, with the day's heat still radiating from the adobe buildings. The mercados were doing their heaviest business of the day. The Mexicans were taking their paseo around the plaza; the youths and men strolling one way, the shy girls and their mothers or dueñas going the other, with lots of admiring glances and swift smiles as they passed.

A nice custom, Nathaniel thought as he slipped into the stream. One he could enjoy himself, until he met the stage. Pretty dark girls, bronze, short, much too wide of beam for his taste, wearing snowy white blusas. His eyes followed one slender, dark beauty as she passed, and as he turned he spotted the sad-eyed hombre from the cantina a dozen or so paces behind.

Dusk settled into blue desert night and candles and lamps glowed behind the barred windows of the tan city.

He turned west off the plaza, toward the Butterfield office, onto a clay street that led toward Tucson Mountain and the last light of the sun.

"Next Prescott stage's due at six in the mornin'," said the clerk behind the grilled window. "They've gotta cross that Salt River Desert by night or kill the horses." The light from the whale-oil lamp bobbed off his Adam's apple.

Someone entered and stood behind Nathaniel.

"I'll meet that one. I think my wife and children are on it." Nathaniel grinned.

"Tall, blue-eyed woman? Little girl and skinny boy? I remember 'em. Sold the tickets," said the clerk proudly. "We're always on time, if not ahead, except if a wheel goes or there's Indian trouble. Six A.M."

Nathaniel turned. The man behind was the hombre. Nathaniel looked at him sharply.

That's one too many, amigo, he thought, and stalked out slowly, waiting for the other to follow. He ambled through hushed streets, narrow in the night, turning randomly. Twice he spotted the sweaty camisa behind. He was being followed, then. Olivera! He walked briskly toward the Santa Rita, with the ghost in his shadows. Shortly before he reached the hotel he backtracked up to the man.

He grabbed a fistful of dirty shirt and banged the man into the wall. He scarcely knew his own strength, a strength built from years of manhandling a one-bottom plow behind a team of Belgians at Concord.

"You working for Olivera?"

"*No hablo inglés.*"

"The hell you don't," Nathaniel snapped, and banged him into the adobe again. The man's head bounced and he shook it dazedly.

"*No hablo—*"

"I've got a message for Olivera, and you damned well better get it to him! Get off my land. Got that? *Get off my land.* And here's another. An eye for an eye and a tooth for a tooth."

Nathaniel banged him into the wall again for an exclamation point.

"I don't talk to Olivera. I talk to Carillo," the man whined.

"You get the message to Olivera," Nathaniel rasped. "And if I catch you or anyone else behind me, you'll wish you were a hundred miles into Sonora." He banged the man again for emphasis, and stalked into the hotel.

Shortly after five the next morning he was pacing the clay street before the Butterfield office. Dawn was slow because of a cloudbank in the east. At twenty to six the dusty stage rolled in, and the horses blew and shook off dust while the driver leaped down and opened the enameled door.

He saw her in the murky light, and hugged her, and slipped his big paw over Charity's little one, and tousled the hair of his boy.

He paused to look at Jonathan. He hadn't paid much attention to his son for so long. He had grown tall, almost a man, and Nathaniel had missed the way the lad's body had filled out and muscled up the last few months.

". . . and I sat up on the box the whole first night. And when we got to the Verde he let me hold the shotgun, and I told him I sure knew how to use it," the boy was saying with a voice that creaked now and then.

They walked in the dawn to the hotel, and Nathaniel felt the joyous presence of the tall woman striding beside him. He saw the cream of her cheek, the softness of her lips as she told him about her talk with the governor. There was some faint perfume about her, maybe from the hotel soap. He saw the wisp of glossy hair that curled over an ear.

"Almost time for breakfast, Papa. I could eat a bear!" yelled the boy as they entered the Santa Rita.

"It's early. Dining room doesn't open till seven. Why don't you kids rest awhile first?" said Nathaniel huskily.

Patience turned to gaze at him. She had heard some eagerness in his voice and now saw it in his face. A certain anticipation stole through her body, even though she was tired.

"Charity, you lie down for a while, dear. You and Jon in your room," she said urgently. "We can't eat now anyway, and I want to be with your father."

CHAPTER 8

Two letters lay on the massive desk in Don Ignacio's study, beneath a fine oil rendering of General Santa Anna, whom Olivera had served as adjutant in his youth, and later as governor of Sonora.

The letters had been brought from Arivaca an hour before by an ancient vaquero who drove the phaeton there weekly for mail and supplies. One was from Mendoza; the other was from el gobernador himself, Major Canfield.

Ignacio grudgingly admired the man's tact. Canfield wrote that the Hapgoods had petitioned him for protection. He had searched diligently for records of the Olivera grant and had found none. If there was land in dispute, it would be up to Señor Olivera to pursue the matter in the territorial courts, and produce title. In any case, Olivera should protect himself by recording his Spanish grant properly. . . .

It was only in the final sentences that Ignacio discovered some steel inside the kid glove. Canfield wrote that he was sending the Hapgoods back to their ranch under his personal protection. He would hold Olivera personally responsible for any harm that befell them.

With what? Ignacio wondered. *A platoon from Lowell?*

But he was wary. He didn't like the circumstances at all. He was a Mexican and a patriot who had fought the

Norte Americanos in the war, and now he was answering to these foreigners because a survey party had drawn an invisible line separating Arizona from Sonora, a few hundred yards south of his casa. Jesus, Mary, Joseph, it was a hard thing, sundering his great holding in two!

He could dispose of these Hapgoods easily enough, but there would be a hundred more Hapgoods in his own lifetime. The gringos were coming. The green and white and red flag fluttered defiantly from his flagpole, as it had for twenty years since the purchase. But how long would it still fly?

"Bad news, Papa?"

"No." He smiled sardonically. "It seems we are to have neighbors."

She beamed. She always looked younger when she smiled, he thought. She was too solemn. She had never had sisters or brothers, and had become an adult too soon. And worse, there were no suitors here in the wilderness of the norte. She wasn't so plain, after all. He had seen her smile sometimes at the capitán, inviting and daring him. What sort of hombre was he to resist that? And the dowry?

"Maria, find me Castillo-Armas, *por favor.*"

He dipped a cup of cool water from the sweating olla. It was hot, even here behind three feet of adobe wall.

"Capitán! Come in! Don't go, Maria. There are things for the three of us to discuss."

He handed the letters to the capitán, who studied them.

"What do you intend to do?" he asked at last.

Ignacio sighed. "There's a time to be a lion and a time to be a fox," he growled. "Now we must be foxes."

The thought rankled him. The very name, Hacienda del Leon, a name deliberately selected by Patricio Olivera in 1762 to remind his heirs of certain eternal verities, cried out against it.

The capitán waited, knowing that Ignacio would reveal himself as soon as he collected his thoughts.

"We mustn't pick a fight with the Norte Americanos," he began. "For the moment, our pistoleros are a stronger force, but it is their land and their cavalry will soon control the Apaches."

"Power speaks loudly," the capitán reminded him.

The patrón sighed. "These Hapgoods may not actually be on our land."

The capitán was amazed. "Why, Don Ignacio, they're on the rincon and the western mountains. How can you say—"

"I know, I know," Ignacio growled. "The Olivera grant is what we say it is with our pistoleros. But the royal grant my grandfather received in 1799 is something else."

The capitán hid his astonishment. Not in three years' service to this family had he heard of it.

"The fact is," Ignacio explained, "we don't know where the boundaries run. We possess the Altar Valley, but the Bourbon kings of Spain reserved the mountains on either side.

"You see, Pedro, gold had been discovered at Oro Blanco east of here. The ministers of the crown were jingling Oro Blanco gold in their hands when Patricio Olivera petitioned them.

"They decided if there was gold to the east, there might also be gold in the west, so they reserved the Baboquivari Range for the crown.

"Patricio wanted the Altar Valley from ridge to ridge, as was the custom. Nothing had been surveyed then, and ridges were the best landmarks.

"He built this casa in 1762, but it wasn't until he was

an old man, in 1799, that the crown granted him this valley.

"The language dismayed Patricio. It said that the boundary was to be one league—three English miles—inward from the ridges. The crown believed such lines would give us the lowlands and reserve the mountains and foothills for the royal treasury."

"I see," mused the capitán. "Not very practical, this abstraction concocted across the ocean."

"It was impossible!" Ignacio snapped. "The ridges—what there are of them—run every which way! Lines don't exist! We have no east and west boundaries, other than what we enforce with fusil and pistola."

He smiled slowly.

"The grant was a piece of parchment anyway. The frontera imposed its own law of survival. The niceties had no meaning here!"

"The grant—it is not recorded with the Norte Americanos?" the capitán asked, knowing the answer.

"No! And it never will be!" Ignacio replied savagely.

The capitán knew why.

"I fought them first in Texas, then with Santa Anna, from here to Vera Cruz. And then they *bought* me!" he growled.

The memory was bitter. At first the Gadsden Purchase had meant little; some of the northern lands would become part of the United States. There were even advantages in it. . . . But then the Boundary Commission came, and drew a line just south of the Hacienda del Leon. The surveyors showed him the border and the five-mile posts, the relentless border that severed him from his patria, his people, his state, those of his tongue, and even his church.

"It was the worst blow of my life," he muttered. "No,

the second worst. The worst was when La Doña Luz died. That was the worst."

He glanced at the oval portrait of a handsome dark woman over the fireplace, and sighed.

The capitán arose. "These Americanos have a saying that they get from the English—possession is nine tenths of the law. Don Ignacio, whatever you've controlled for so long is your own, so far as their courts are concerned. So why don't I take the pistoleros there and keep the Hapgoods away when they come?"

Ignacio ran a hand through wiry gray hair.

"It's not a military matter," he said. "The first incident, we'd be driven from here. My hacienda hangs in balance, Capitán! Times are changing!"

"I would like neighbors," Maria said firmly. "We have none."

"We need new tactics now," Ignacio continued, ignoring her. "The Hapgoods are coming under the protection of Major Canfield. Shall we kill them? Mother of God, the gringos would slaughter all of us."

"You will let them stay, then!" Maria exclaimed.

Ignacio glared.

"Let them nibble our borders? No, no, no. Capitán, go there and scorch the earth, yes? When they return, let them find their casita razed to the ground. Get Ramirez and Navarro to help. Burn the corrals. Drive their cattle to the Papagoes—keep none. We are not thieves. Ditch the ciénaga so it drains dry. Burn what's left. The Romans did it to Carthage, and Carthage died. Do it pronto before the Hapgoods return, and they'll give up and leave without any pressure from us!"

The capitán was reluctant. "It's a fine casita, Don Ignacio. The hacienda could put that rancho to good use."

"We've managed without it for over a century," Ignacio said sardonically. "Demolish it."

The capitán cleared his throat.

"Patrón. A small question. Why not just record the royal grant with their officials? The lawyers could define the boundaries without ever going to court. Why risk trouble with the gobernador in Prescott, or Washington?"

Ignacio stared moodily at the dark desk, and glanced at Santa Anna, staring imperiously from his gilded frame.

"Maria—Pedro—I'm not a practical man. How can I say all this? To you alone I'll speak, and you alone will understand."

He paced the room as he talked.

"Maria, you are a Mexican, yes? Baptised in the holy faith. Spanish by tongue. Reared to a certain womanhood —our Mexican women are loved so much more than the ones in the norte. It is because we honor the Virgin . . ."

He paused, struggling.

"I can't record the Olivera grant with them. Because then—we would be Americanos. It is simple, yes? Record the deeds, let their officials come here to this soil, run up their flag. I can't. When I was a youth I fought. . . . It's not so simple. Pedro, amigo, we are Mexicans in our bone and blood and spirit. You fought for our flag! Did you do it for nothing? Shall I take that old grant, ten pages of fine script on parchment paper, up to them and have them record it? God forbid!"

The capitán listened, watching Maria all the while. She gazed into his eyes, smiled, and glanced away.

"I've watched their culture," Ignacio continued. "They've a genius for manufacture and commerce, and are a vital people. A race of traders, if not pirates. I admire it! But I don't want it in Mexico. We have a different way, what we call our haciendas. Our peasants have a hard life, but they're secure. We don't throw them out the way the gringo factories do when they're old. They have their little tasks, and feel useful to their last days. They sew, or watch the niños, or mend harness.

"I send for the padre to baptise them and bury them and hear their confessions. I call the doctors. I make sure they never lack for food or a roof over their heads as long as they live. Shall we change all that? Like the rootless ones in the United States? I'm no democrat; I'd never abandon my poor little ones to plots where they'd starve, or condemn them to the cities where they'd corrupt themselves. Ah! No . . . borrow from the northerners, yes. But each Sunday in my pew I pray to God for Mexico . . ."

Ignacio paused, and then seemed to shrink down inside himself. He was not used to baring so much, even to his dearest ones.

"I agree with you," said the capitán simply. "What more is there to say? We can only keep our ways in this alien land or leave it."

He gazed gently at Maria, as if seeing her for the first time, seeing beyond those unfortunate jowls to the thoughtful eyes and young smooth skin, and the figure gracefully lifting and filling the blue linen of her dress.

"I'll leave with Juanito after lunch," he said brusquely. "With the vaqueros, that's all I'll need. It'll take a few days."

He ordered three horses from the corrals, and the tools. Then he had a better idea, and had the twelve-pound cannon hitched to a good draft horse, along with balls and powder. He would teach Juanito a thing or two about cannoneering, and save some hard labor as well.

Don Ignacio watched from his window, amused.

"Maria! Look at your capitán. He's taking the cannon and Juanito. Good thinking! He'll make sport of the casita, and teach the boy a thing or two!"

They watched from the windows as the officer and boy left upon the mission of destruction.

"A policy like this might serve the Oliveras through my lifetime and beyond." Ignacio beamed. "Being the fox now."

He looked suddenly at Maria, and spoke gently.

"Ah, little Maria, it will soon be in your hands, this blood, this domain. I pray God he will bless you with a husband and children soon."

She blushed and stared out upon the empty plaza. Then she ran to her room and closed the door.

She knelt before an exquisite image of the smiling Virgin.

"Santa Maria, Madre y Reina Nuestra, intercede for me. Let my Pedro be safe. Let those Hapgoods be safe, too. Let them not shoot or fight if they should meet. Santa Maria, turn your son's eyes to my Pedro, and bless him. Let my Pedro notice me. I am plain and he does not see me inside. Oh *Madre mía, muchas gracias . . .*"

She rose, bitterly.

Augustin Talliferro watched, too, as the capitán and muchacho rumbled out of the plaza and headed north. Then Talliferro saddled quickly, choosing a black mare, the fastest in Ignacio's stable. If there was wealth to be had, he wanted it.

Augustin Talliferro lay upon the ridge east of the Hapgood casita, studying the place through his brass spyglass. The big mules were near the ciénaga, and the fine freight wagon. What a price they'd fetch in Hermosillo!

There were horses in the corrals, so the vaqueros were there. Talliferro was disappointed. He had hoped to slip into the rancho and steal the Winchester repeaters. But now it would be difficult—unless he killed them. . . .

He folded the spyglass, which he had possessed ever since he jumped ship in Vera Cruz. The instrument actually belonged to the master of that Majorcan four-mast bark, but Talliferro had pilfered it at the last moment. The bark plied a trade route from Mediterranean ports to Mexico, but had acquired a reputation as a bad-luck ship because a man had been lost at sea during each of the three crossings in which Talliferro was mate.

He had, in fact, knocked them senseless during his night rounds and eased them overboard. Each had possessed certain valuables, and these Talliferro had locked in a watertight chest he kept in the bilge.

But in Vera Cruz he had made a mistake, and had sold to a jeweler a solid-gold crucifix that bore the victim's name on the back. He had hidden in the barrios while the police and the master hunted him, and then had fled into the interior.

The Hapgood rancho was tranquil in the late afternoon sun. The horses dozed. There was no cook smoke. Near the ciénaga a dozen cattle chewed their cud.

The crawling cannon and cassion wouldn't arrive until the next day, he knew. The capitán and Juanito would have slow going dragging that siege gun, cannon balls, and powder behind the big draft horse. It had been easy to loop ahead of them on Ignacio's fast mare.

And now he was gazing down on the Hapgood wealth. Cattle! Wagons! Maybe gold in the casita! He was sick of dog's wages and Ignacio's dirty work.

He studied the place for an hour, with the patience of his trade. Then he watched the bandy-legged vaquero emerge from the casita, stretch, and walk to the corrals.

Talliferro picked up his rifle silently, propped himself on his elbows, and lined the sights on the vaquero's chest. He followed the man with his sights while his finger spasmed on the trigger, not quite hard enough to fire the weapon.

He grinned. It would be easy to get one. He swung the

barrel to the door, the windows, the outhouse. Easy! He pulled the barrel back from the crack in the ridge rock and studied his position. He cleared away some piñon brush that might make noise if he retreated suddenly. He moved a boulder that might mean a ricochet. Care! Detail! Patience! These had allowed him to ply his trade for years without harm.

He toyed with the notion of killing the vaqueros. Then he'd be free to steal what he could and get away before the capitán arrived. It was tempting. He could cache the loot, tie the bodies over the horses, like sacks of grain, and tell the capitán that Hapgood had done it, and he had arrived too late to help.

But he doubted the capitán would believe it. He or Ignacio would only ask him what he was doing there. And long discipline made Talliferro wary of improvised plans. Worse, Olivera might send a whole army of pistoleros after the Hapgoods, gather all the possessions and wealth before Talliferro could get to them.

No. It would be better to leave here quietly or wait to see what the capitán would do. He could not reveal himself to the vaqueros below. They loathed him; they all did, and he lived in total isolation at the hacienda. They might even try to kill him. Talliferro smiled. That would take some doing. Those vaqueros would be dead from his fast pistola before they could even unholster their own.

Talliferro slithered back to his black mare, and mounted silently. He had seen a trail from the head of Hapgood Canyon rising steeply toward the great peak, and now he would explore it. He liked to learn all he could about a place—and its escape routes—before a kill. He rode quietly, keeping the mare away from gravel. He had learned to move like a shadow and blend with the land. His eyes darted everywhere, seeing everything.

El patrón was paying him nothing—dirt—to terrorize

the Papagoes, he thought bitterly. He had tolerated it for years. Even put up with that vainglorious capitán.

These Hapgoods, now. They were no frontier riffraff. They had dinero. New Winchesters at the casita. A gold ring with a diamond upon the finger of the madam. Maybe five hundred cows and calves in these mountains. Yes, easily that. He rolled the figure through his mind, and found it fragrant. There was browse here for that many. He could gather them up, a few at a time, and sell them!

A few to Hermosillo. A few to Tucson. A few to Oro Blanco, or Arivaca, or Nogales. There'd be wealth in that casita, too. Silverware, perhaps. Double eagles hidden away. The Hapgoods had been driven out with nothing. It was all there, their entire wealth!

It would be enough for the rest of his life. He could return to Majorca in style and have a villa on the sea. He would put everything in the freight wagon and drive south. Then he would sell it all, including the wagon, and set sail. And if the Hapgoods returned, he would feed them to the turkey vultures.

The trail rose steeply before him. It had seen heavy use. There was abundant cattle and horse sign. It was the avenida to the Hapgood ranges; any fool could see that. He would find where the rest of the cattle were, and figure how to spirit them to markets.

The climb was breath-taking. He caught glimpses of the Hapgood rancho far below, through openings in the piñon. It was cooler here. The trail branched near the sheer massif of Baboquivari. He let the mare blow, and took the west trail, which showed signs of more use.

He rode silently out upon the western shoulder in the last low sun. Above him was talus, and above that was the massif, flaming in the setting sun. Below was a sloping plateau—with some cattle and horses on it. He stared at the horses. He had seen them before. And some had fresh saddle marks on them.

Excited, he eased back to the deep shadow of a juniper copse and watched. Nothing. The horses below caught his scent, and stared at him. Talliferro was uneasy.

Then he saw movement at the very top of the talus where a gigantic rock had fallen from the façade. The Hapgood muchacho! The boy staggered down the talus carrying two heavy buckets, emptied water into a natural tanque near the horses, and repeated the journey thrice more.

So! They were here! And there was water here! And a cave, or protected ledge. The hombre and dama, the señorita, too. He could kill the muchacho now. But that talus . . . Any approach would be difficult. No cover. It was a fortress, with water.

He grinned. Hapgoods on this side of the rancho. El Capitán coming up on the other side. It would be a great show, and he would pick up the pieces, the horses, cattle, everything. And he would have a cave to hide in, along with his loot.

Talliferro eased downslope in the dusk, delighted, and made camp at a level place he had noticed. Mañana he would be rich, and many would be dead.

CHAPTER 9

Nathaniel eyed the cave uneasily. The rains usually came
on San Juan's Day, June 24. The pool at the back of the
cave was obviously replenished by rainwater rushing
down the sheer face of Baboquivari. He studied the walls
carefully for a high-water mark and found it exactly at
the height of the entrance floor. When the storms came,
the cave would fill up, and they would be in danger of
drowning. That's what Night Hawk was talking about!

They had perhaps a week, maybe a few days more, to
round up the cattle and move them to Brother Pierre's.
Once the rains came, the cattle on the rincon would cease
watering at the ciénaga. They would spread out and
it would be virtually impossible to gather them until the
arroyos dried again. There were still some cattle watering
here in the mountains, God knows where. Some had
shown up at the cave, but others were visible on distant
ridges.

He searched for some alternative, some ledge or shelter
where they would be safe and dry. He found none. If
they were forced out of the cave during a violent storm,
they would step into cannonades of thunder and balls of
lightning and unspeakable violence. He had been in the
mountains during an electrical storm that first September, and he never wanted to go through an ordeal like

that again. If the rains came early, they wouldn't even have a week, he thought. Each day's delay put them into deeper jeopardy.

The rains were a real menace: they threatened his life here at the cave, and threatened to put his cattle forever out of reach.

Another worry clawed at him. To move those cattle from the rincon to Pierre's, he'd have to push them right past those vaqueros in his casa. That meant he had to get those hombres out of his ranch home fast. Tomorrow! And he would have to use stealth, guile, or whatever force he could manage. Armed force dismayed him. He wished there were some other way—talk, money, law, courts. But he was alone in the desert against men who would shoot strangers. It made a man appreciate the mechanics of civilization, he thought. He knew he was afraid. And not just for himself. He would need Jon to back him, and that troubled him all the more.

"Patience, things are going to happen fast now. The next step is to go home and get our cattle to safety."

She turned to gaze at him, knowing.

"It may be the hardest part," he said quietly.

She read the unspoken thoughts in his face, and then glanced at Jonathan, and then into the murk of the cave. She said nothing for a while, and then stood close to him and put a gentle hand on his shoulder.

"I'll cover you with the buffalo gun." She grinned.

Long before dawn, while the moon bathed the dry mountains, Nathaniel awakened his family, saddled their horses, and checked weapons.

They rode down the slope, with Charity clinging sleepily to her mother. They tied the horses above their canyon and Patience wrapped the sleepy child in a blanket and told her to stay right there with the horses.

The casa glowed white in the moonlight. The horses in

the corral stared at the intruders, and one began to pace.
Nathaniel squeezed his bride's hand.

"If you must shoot, rest the barrel on something solid
and keep the stock tight against your shoulder. If it's not
tight, it could hurt," he whispered.

She parted from her men carrying the Sharps, a canteen, and jerky. Nathaniel insisted that each of them be
able to endure a long wait in the sun. She slipped behind
the parapet of the stronghold, settled in shadow, and
dreaded the dawn.

Nathaniel and Jon crept toward the rear of the casa,
clinging to the shadows.

"Step lightly into the wagon, son. Don't let it creak.
Pick one of the big knotholes. Have your water and your
cartridges, now?"

"Yes, and jerky," the boy whispered, easing himself
into the bowels of the wagon, behind two-inch plank.

Then Nathaniel eased himself into the adobe two-holer
and sat down. He had no very clever plan. His only object
was to capture the vaqueros before they forted up behind
the loopholes of the casa. If that happened, he and Jon
and Patience would be pinned down all day. He dreaded
the next hours, but it was too late to pull back. They were
committed.

Dawn came slowly, and Nathaniel fidgeted in that
odorous place. The murk shifted to gray, and at last he
heard muffled movement in the casa. The first rays of sun
struck the high shoulder of Baboquivari. He smelled mesquite smoke, then tortillas. Then the door on the far side
was unbolted. He heard footfalls. He tensed as the door
creaked open and the bulk of a man pushed in.

"*Manos arriba!*" he hissed. The hombre slowly lifted his
hands. He was unarmed.

"Take off your boots," he hissed. He lacked the words.

"*Zapatos, zapatos!*" he snapped. The man understood, and slowly lowered his hands and pulled them off.

"Turn around." The hombre saw the corkscrew motion of Nathaniel's hand, and turned.

"*Manos!*" The hands eased back and Nathaniel whipped a thong around the wrists.

Then the waiting began again. The sun slid down the western ridge, and the heat came up. Nathaniel heard the wagon creak. Jon was getting restless. He wondered how Patience was faring. At least she had shade.

Inside the casa, the old vaquero Navarro, who had lived long with nature, felt a subtle change that he could not have expressed in words. Perhaps the birds were a little shrill. The rhythms were wrong. And his amigo did not return.

Navarro quietly bolted the door and picked up one of the Winchesters. It felt good; the lever action and brass cartridges would make great red holes. So then. They had Ramirez.

He studied the scene from a loophole, moving from rock to rock, tree to tree. He saw the blue barrel projecting from the wagon. Three knotholes but one barrel. One hombre. Another in the tocado, holding Ramirez. Maybe a third back there behind the ciénaga; the light was bad.

Navarro eased the barrel into the loophole and drew a careful bead on a wagon knothole, the one with the rifle in it, and fired. The blast shattered the dawn. Then he sent a slug screaming through the second knothole, then the third.

Nathaniel's heart thudded in the dying echoes. Now they were in a jackpot, thanks to his poor planning.

"Jonathan . . . are you all right?" he asked shakily, concealing his dread.

"I guess." The boy quivered. "He hit the stock of the

carbine and my hand hurts so's I can hardly hold it. But I'm not hit."

"Thank God," Nathaniel cried. "Listen, Jon. Stay clear of those holes!"

"Do you think I'm crazy?" the boy retorted. "I'm stuck, Pa. I can't go over the rear. He'd get me."

"Jon. I'm going to yell and go in and draw his attention from you. When I go, you go too. Forward, up to the casa where it's safe. Forward. Got that?"

Nathaniel felt shaky. Blood pounded in his temples. He was plain scared, and he knew the boy was even more so.

Patience heard every word in the quiet morning air. And she, best of all, saw that evil barrel protruding from her casa, the barrel that would kill her husband and son. She rested the octagonal barrel of the Sharps in the crotch of a mesquite log, letting its dead weight steady it.

Trembling, she pushed her shoulder to the butt and sighted down the barrel until the notch was exactly upon the loophole. Then she squeezed. There was a whoom and a jolt. The fifty-caliber ball smashed into the shutter just an inch from the loophole and sent a holocaust of splinters and lead into the casa. She rammed home a new charge and ball.

Nathaniel leaped when he heard the boom. He drove a shot from his Colt toward the loophole, and saw the barrel waver and lift.

"Now, Jon!" he yelled as he bolted into the open. Jon vaulted from the wagon and reached the casa wall a moment behind Nathaniel.

Inside, a mass of slivers and bits of lead smashed into Navarro's face and stung his eyes. Tears welled, and he couldn't see. A flood oozed from one eye while the other puffed up and closed. He rubbed his face, feeling blood, and sank to the floor helplessly, terrified that he'd be blind.

Nathaniel raced to the front of the house and found a shutter open. He fired wildly into the casa, and then popped into the window, primed for another.

"No! No!" screamed Navarro. "*No tire!*"

Nathaniel lowered the Colt. It was over, then. He sagged weakly against the window frame while Navarro wept and rubbed his eyes. Jon came, pale and trembling, and gathered the weapons while he kept an eye on Navarro. Patience came, while Nathaniel brought Ramirez from the outhouse.

"We're all okay," he said quietly as she ran to him. Something released in her, like river ice breaking in a thaw, and she lowered the buffalo gun mutely.

"We've got to get Charity," she whispered.

"I'll come and lead the horses," Nathaniel said. "Jon can handle these men. One's hurt some, and I want to have a look first."

He squatted beside the weeping Navarro. There were pinpricks and lacerations on his forehead and cheeks. One eye was shut; the other was red and oozing tears. Nathaniel got cool water and bathed the bronze face. The man's lenses seemed to be intact, even if the eyes were inflamed. He would see soon.

Nathaniel felt sorry. But his momentary guilt vanished when he remembered that this hombre had blasted three shots into the wagon. War, even this little war in the canyon, didn't seem immoral; it was just fitful violence coming from men who couldn't compromise or negotiate.

They walked up the trail somberly, neither saying a word. Nathaniel relived the struggle along the way, cursing himself. He had been dumb, a greenhorn, to put his son in the wagon where he was trapped, and to hide himself in an outhouse with the only door facing into the loopholes of the casa. They could have pinned him down forever, and Jon could have broiled to death in the sun.

They found Charity sitting in Cotton Mather's saddle. The reins were broken and the gelding grazed some yards from the other horses. There were dried tears on Charity's cheeks.

"What happened, dear?" Patience asked.

"I saw a man."

"A man? What did you do?"

"I was afraid, so I got up on Cotton. Then he pulled and ran from the man."

"Where was this man? Was he an Indian?"

"There"—she pointed twenty feet away—"and the horses all looked at him."

Nathaniel found prints. A man with small boots had stood just a few feet from Charity.

"God only knows who," he said gravely. The edgy horses probably saved the child, he thought. No one would ever know for sure. So, then. Another life jeopardized by his folly.

Patience closed her eyes a moment and then turned silently to Nathaniel with a question in her face. Was it worth it? This risk and danger and pain? He saw her eyes and understood, and sighed. He had no answer.

She hugged the child and then they trudged home with the horses. At least they had a home to go to now.

It was not yet nine.

Patience began at once to establish that certain communion a woman has with her house. She scrubbed and swept and watered her browning hollyhocks. She examined shelves and stores. She pulled the blankets and beat dust from them in the sun.

Jonathan idly guarded the vaqueros while Nathaniel tended the animals and troubled his mind with the next steps. He couldn't let the vaqueros go—not just yet. They'd race back to the hacienda before he could get his cattle out of Olivera's reach. Olivera could have his pistoleros back here by tomorrow evening if they rode hard.

Time seemed to be the key to everything. Actually, Nathaniel thought, the gather would be easy. By dusk, nearly all of his cattle in the rincon would have come up here to the ciénaga for water. There were a dozen dozing here now. If there were stragglers, he'd just leave them behind. He and Jon could move the herd to the monk's pasture by dawn.

He swung the corral gate on its rawhide hinges and boogered the cattle into the pen. Four Olivera horses were in there, fine short-coupled animals. There were two he liked, and then an ironic idea crossed his mind. He smiled, and forked them some hay.

After they got those cattle to the monk's canyon, then what? How was he going to protect Patience and Charity? Should they all go, and abandon the hard-won casa? Would Canfield's letter to Olivera help now, and keep the Mexican at bay? He worried the problem while he worked, and didn't come up with much of a solution. Whatever he did, it wasn't going to be a tea party.

"Patience . . ." He came up behind her as she peeled onions, and slipped his hands around her waist. She stood straight and smiled. "Patience, I've been thinking."

She knew that was his usual prelude to an announcement.

"I think I'll take Jon with me and push the cattle west as soon as the moon's up. Before we go, we'll take these hombres to the foot of the canyon and let them go. The problem is, you won't be safe here alone—"

"Yes we will," she said.

"Why don't you and Charity come with us? Don't want to leave you here."

"We've got the old Colt back, and I can close shutters, and I'll have some fresh bread cooling when you return." She smiled.

He surrendered. "Well, we'll probably be back before . . . Look. I'll leave a Winchester. We've got three now."

"I'll miss you tonight," she laughed. "I was planning on a homecoming—just for you and me!"

She sure wasn't making it easy for him, he thought.

But Patience was home, and home was where she intended to stay. It was the reason she accepted the dangers and privations of the wilderness. There, in her tiny civilized spot, her garden grew, and along with it, her dreams.

She laughed, and hummed, and scrubbed a bucket, and trotted out to milk Jezebel, poor thing, if she still had milk.

Midafternoon, a large bunch of cattle drifted in, and Nathaniel penned them. There were calves that needed branding, and some doctoring to do.

"Jon, bring the vaqueros where we can keep an eye on them, and then let's get to work on these cattle. We'll do some branding!"

Jon saddled while Nathaniel built a mesquite fire and heated their iron. The Mexicans watched quietly on the fence. The one held cold compresses to one eye, but could use the other.

Jonathan was no cowboy, and he thundered furiously around the corral while the calves squirted out from him. His rope sailed and bounced off tails and dirt and noses, while the vaqueros watched pensively. The boy was barely concealing his temper, and Nathaniel grew irritated by the spectacle. Then, as Jon coiled his rope, Ramirez volunteered to help.

Nathaniel debated the matter. He wore his Colt, and Jon had his carbine on his horse. But that wasn't the point. These old Mexican cowboys weren't gunmen, he knew. They were just a couple of vaqueros waiting to go home. Probably couldn't stand the spectacle, he thought dourly.

"Sure," he said. "We'd be grateful."

The vaquero threw a saddle over an Olivera horse and released his finely woven reata and whirled it gracefully a few times. Then it settled magically over the neck of a white-faced calf. Jon bulldogged the calf while the vaquero's horse backed up until the slender line was taut. In an instant Nathaniel's brand scorched into the thigh and the calf was loose, bawling madly, looking for his mama.

The afternoon's work suddenly went smoothly. The vaquero moved fluidly through the herd, his horse pivoting right or left, bolting forward or drawing to a halt without a visible command from the horseman.

One by one the calves were cut out and branded. Never once did the snaking, whirling reata miss its mark.

By dusk there were fifty-eight critters in the pens and no more coming up the canyon. Nathaniel called a halt, and Patience, wise to country ways, laid out enough steaming food for ten and watched it all vanish.

"*Muchas gracias,*" Nathaniel said to the one who had helped. "Jon, tell them I have a message for Olivera. We're here peaceably. If he wants trouble, we'll return it, an eye for an eye."

Jonathan translated.

"Now tell them I'm taking them to the foot of the canyon and releasing them. I'll give them their carbines back and enough ammunition to get them to the hacienda safely. Tell them this is our patented land, and there'll be plenty of trouble if they return."

Both vaqueros nodded.

"Tell Olivera I'm keeping two horses. That's my price for renting the casa, and also the price of my hay."

He laughed.

The four saddled in the cool of the evening and rode

down to the rincon. Nathaniel quietly handed the carbines to the vaqueros, and offered his hand.

"Adios," said one, taking it. Then they plunged south, into the murk of night. Father and son listened to them until there was only the sound of the crickets, and then rode home.

When the moon rose, they wearily lined the milling cattle into a trail herd and headed up the mountain. To these cattle they would add the few at the cave. In a few weeks, if Canfield's letter to Olivera had the intended effect, perhaps they could bring the cattle home again. It had been a long day, and wasn't over yet.

Patience listened to them a long while, but at last the night was quiet. She wanted the cool night air in the house, but instead bolted the door and shutters, checked her weapons, put Charity to bed, and drifted into deep sleep. Home at last.

CHAPTER 10

It was well after noon the next day before the capitán and Juanito rode into Hapgood Canyon with their twelve-pounder.

Patience heard the clatter long before any figures rounded the bend below, and to her untrained ear it sounded like the approach of a whole army. She might close the shutters and survive against one or two; but against so many pistoleros she could only run.

She grabbed Charity and the carbine and raced to the stronghold behind the ciénaga. Poor little girl, she thought—one terror after another, without end.

She saw the capitán, the one who had whipped Nathaniel, ride idly across the meadow, while another one, with a big black cannon, rattled up behind. She raised her carbine, ready to shoot if she must.

The capitán stared at the corral, saw only two of the Olivera horses there, and rode to the casa.

"*Hola*, Ramirez! Navarro!"

Silence echoed back. He dismounted and wandered through the casa and found nothing amiss. Some soup was heating.

The compadres were out riding somewhere, he decided. Perhaps checking the Hapgood cattle. The Winchesters were gone. It was wise of the vaqueros to take such excellent weapons with them. Well, then, he was going to spoil their soup!

There'd be no difficulty. He would level the casa before the Hapgoods returned, exactly as Don Ignacio wished.

"*Saludos, muchachos!*" he called one last time, and then rode back to Juanito.

"Now, my mozo, we'll have a little lesson in cannoneering. This old lady is a muzzle loader, so we'll stuff the powder and ball down her throat, like this."

He rammed the ball home and cranked the muzzle until he knew the first shot would overreach.

"This one will probably go too far," he explained. "But then we can tell how much to raise the barrel."

He fussed with the black engine until he was satisfied.

"Now, muchacho, put the punk to the touch hole!"

The piece whoomed and leaped backward, knocking down Juanito and bruising him. The ball thudded beyond the casa, raising a geyser of dirt and rock. Patience involuntarily screamed at the violence, but her cry was lost in the echoes.

"Don't stand behind her, you ignoramus! Now raise the muzzle—that's right—observe the angle. You should have it now. And remember, when you're at war, take cover, and hold your ears."

Juanito rammed the second ball home the way el capitán had done it. Then he danced to one side and touched the punk to the fateful hole, and leaped aside as she roared. This time the ball slammed hard into the Hapgoods' bedroom, across a corner, so that the roof caved in and the shutters flew off the windows. A ball of dust enveloped the building.

"*Muy bueno, muchacho!* You'll learn! Now then, a little to the left. Turn the whole carriage. We'll put this ball right through the door!"

Patience bit her lip and suppressed tears. She covered

Charity with her skirts and lay astride the child, shielding her with her own body.

There was horror now. The third ball roared into the building and the roof seemed to balloon up and then collapse into rubble and dust. The fourth ball thundered through the kitchen, and in that instant Patience saw cans, silverware, bags, pots, and stovepipe screaming every direction in the yellow haze. There was a column of yellow dust now, rising high above the casa and rolling out to the edges of the canyon.

The fifth ball disintegrated the children's room, and the explosion lifted a straw pallet high into the air, where it hung for a long moment before settling softly down. The mud walls flew apart, and long after the sound echoed away bits and pieces of adobe dropped, and shutters rattled to the ground. The sixth ball smashed a rear wall and caught a corner of the outhouse. The ocotillo ramada that Nathaniel had lovingly built for Patience sagged, and slid drunkenly to earth. Rolling noise echoed down the canyon, and the place choked with opaque dust.

"Oh, there's not much left of it now, muchacho. Save the balls. War is hell, yes? And glory, too, when the banners fly before you. . . ." There was a strange light in the capitán's eyes.

"I fired these very ladies against the Norte Americanos during the war of 1847. I saw the balls drop among them, and then they dropped by the dozens. Ah, Juanito, have you ever had a day like this in all your life? It is one you'll remember!"

"No, Capitán," said the smoke-blackened youth wearily. "It's hard work. The balls do not go easily down her throat, and sometimes I have to bang them hard. I think I want to be a pistolero."

"Well, muchacho, one last shot anyway. We'll see what you've learned. I'll watch and say nothing! Hit that freight wagon squarely, over there to the left, and I'll give you a peso out of my own pocket, Juanito."

A peso! The boy began to jimmy the barrel around to the left but burned his hands on the smoking metal. Then he lifted the carriage tongue around, and sighted up toward the distant wagon, even farther away than the casa. *Bueno.* He had her aiming right. It faced the wagon. It faced the overhanging ledge beyond, near the ciénaga, where boulders and logs were piled into a parapet.

The wagon was back a little so he would have to lower the barrel. One notch, two, three. Ah, now she was just right! The freight wagon would fly to bits! No. Three notches weren't enough, and he lowered the barrel one more.

Juanito packed down the powder. A little extra for the wagon. And rammed home the ball, tight against the powder. He sighted again. A peso! And then, his heart pounding, he touched the punk to the hole and danced aside.

The twelve-pounder leaped, and the ball snarled high over the wagon and smashed into the earth just fifteen feet from where Patience Hope Hapgood covered her daughter with her own soft flesh behind the parapet.

The explosion rammed up from the earth and slammed into her stomach and chest and legs. Then the concussion ripped logs and rock loose above her, and tumbled it down on her. Her ears and eyes and mind, insulted by pressure and noise and holocaust, refused to hear or see or think, and she began to hurt everywhere, in her lungs and heart and head and bones as well as her skin and feet and fingers. Charity screamed.

Then she could see again, and there was nothing but opaque dust swirling around her. She felt dizzy and her ears rang. The child squirmed and began to vomit. She felt herself becoming sick, and to keep down the gorge she screamed. She screamed again, and cuddled Charity, and screamed.

～～～   ～～～

Nathaniel and Jonathan dozed in the saddle as their geldings picked their way toward Baboquivari. They had breakfasted with the good monk and then hurried home. They were both beyond the limit of their endurance: the dawn fight at the casa, the branding, and the night drive to the monk's canyon were more than their bodies could take without rest. Nathaniel knew he should be alert but his weariness was beyond control, so he rocked and nodded as Cotton plodded home. Jonathan was even worse off and once had barely caught himself as he slid off the saddle.

Near their canyon, where the trail dropped fast, Nathaniel heard a thump, a muffled thump that didn't sound at all like thunder. It bothered him, but he was too tired to think about it.

There were more thumps, louder now. A breeze brought a faint acrid smell to his nostrils. Some thought clawed at him, but he couldn't get it into words. He was awake and worried. There was dust ahead, yellow in the sun, rising in a column from his canyon, his *home*.

"Come on, Jon! We're going out on the shoulder where we can see!"

He spurred the bay to the right and rode recklessly out along the western arm of Baboquivari, leaping rock and twisting through ocotillo. Cotton wasn't fast enough for Nathaniel's tearing fear, so he leaped off, pulled the Winchester, and raced toward the rimrock, tearing his pants in cholla and kicking through prickly pear. The boy dogged behind, tired, wheezing, and scared.

At the first overlook they squinted down into a boiling yellow haze and patches of blue smoke. Powder smell was in the breeze. Far below there was no casa. *No home.*

Only rubble and a forlorn wall. Stovepipe glinted where the kitchen had been. Smoke curled from some beams.

Where was Patience? Where was Charity? Far to the south he saw two tiny figures. One walked toward the rubble, and even at that distance he recognized the capitán. The other danced around a toy black cannon in the yellow haze. Nathaniel stood high on the slope, hating, hating in the silence.

"Pa, where are they . . . ?" Jon cried.

Then they heard a scream, thin and piercing as the cry of an eagle across a mountain valley, and even at that great height they knew it was her, and that the cry came from their stronghold, faint and clear in the dirty air.

Nathaniel stomped down the mountain. Crashed through thorny ocotillo. Kicked through rock. Smashed over mesquite. He had to get in range! Had to stop that dot of a man walking toward Patience! He was suddenly all will, full of a terrible ferocity compounded of love, terror, and hatred—hatred for that man with the pistol drawn walking toward Patience Hope Hapgood.

Nathaniel couldn't wait. He was still over three hundred yards from that tiny figure, but he swung his Winchester down savagely and blasted. Then, more sensibly, he rested it on table rock, paused to bring his thumping heart and trembling hands into control, and squeezed, and levered, and squeezed the trigger again. Two puffs of dust ripped the earth near Castillo-Armas. He paused, looked up, and Jonathan whanged a round that whipped past the capitán's ear. The soldier whirled and trotted back toward Juanito and the cannon.

Nathaniel roared down the slope.

"Come on, Jon, we're out of range," he rasped as he stomped down and down. He hawked up a blob of spit and fired it, and stood up tall and cracked a shot at the cannoneer. He spat again and shot again, weaving and bobbing south along the ridge.

Far below, Castillo-Armas cursed the stupid Juanito, who was dancing wildly, afraid of the whining bullets. The capitán dragged the carriage tongue around and eyed the mad mountain.

"Bring the horse!" he screamed at the boy, and then he hitched the animal to the carriage because Juanito was out of his head. A shot splattered gravel, and another whanged off the barrel of the black lady, and a third screamed over the draft horse.

Nathaniel paused in a watercourse to stuff shells into the long Winchester magazine, and then he and Jon plunged down a long gravel slope until they had gained another hundred yards on the cannoneers below. The dots were larger now. He rested the hot barrel in the crook of a saguaro arm and shot, and spat. The bullet streaked across the neck of a horse, leaving a furrow of blood. The horse pitched and screamed and bowled over the small figure that was hanging on to it. Nathaniel's mouth was full of juices, and he spat a gob that sailed far down.

The capitán's whip cracked across the rump of the draft horse and the iron tires of the gun carriage screeched as the cannon began to roll. Juanito leaped to his horse and spurred crazily, but the capitán boarded slowly, keeping his injured animal as calm as possible. Then he drew his dragoon pistol and snapped five shots up the slope to slow the loco hombres above.

"Five, huh!" Nathaniel spat as he listened to the pops from below. Jonathan cracked a shot at the distant capitán, and missed. Then they peppered the retreating figures as they gathered speed and rounded a bend in the canyon and disappeared. The howl of iron tires and the tap of galloping hoofs drifted back to them amid the silence.

The boy and the man stood at the brink of a fifty-foot cliff that formed the canyon wall. It frustrated any movement toward Patience, so they raced south, like trapped lions, until they found a precipitous chute, and skidded down to the canyon floor, and the meadow. They ran, breathlessly, past the rubble, past the wagon, around the ciénaga.

They saw her standing there under the ledge, caked with gray dust. She stood in shadow, scarcely recognizing them, not comprehending she was safe. Charity sat below, snuffling.

"Patience! My God, Patience!" he cried, and enfolded her in the safety of his arms and held her tight. She felt herself coming toward him from a great distance, from some other sphere. She felt strong warm arms around her, and that brought her closer still. Then she was aware she was *here*, and he was here with her, and Jon and Charity, and her own arms reached up around his neck and they clung to him desperately.

Far down the canyon, Juanito spurred his horse crazily, wanting nothing but to escape the canyon of death. Behind him lumbered the draft horse dragging the careening gun carriage. Still farther above was Castillo-Armas, calmly struggling with his wounded gelding.

"Slow down, muchacho, we're safe now!" he yelled to the galloping boy, but the boy didn't listen.

The carriage wheel struck a boulder, and the twelve-pounder tottered crazily and righted itself.

"Juanito! *Alto!*"

But the muchacho had spurred his mount into a flat gallop, and the draft animal thundered along behind.

An iron tire smashed into a low ledge, and the whole carriage lifted up on one wheel, crashed back onto the other wheel, bounced high into a twisting arc, and plunged into the arroyo running alongside the trail, taking the big horse with it. The horse's feet were ripped out from under it and the rotating cannon flipped the horse onto its back as the animal and cannon crashed down into the rock. The horse's neck snapped, and he pawed the air a moment, shuddered, and died. The carriage smashed to an abrupt halt and shattered, while the iron barrel snaked down to the sand of the arroyo bottom and stuck there.

The capitán pulled up and sighed. It would not be necessary to shoot the horse; perhaps it would be better to shoot the muchacho. The boy, who finally halted two hundred yards down, trotted back up, bug-eyed.

"Ah, Juanito, if you were a Federale I would shoot you with the last bullet in my pistola," the capitán growled. "But you aren't a Federale."

They limped quietly away from the devastation and out upon the rincon.

"I wonder where those bone-headed vaqueros were when we needed them," the capitán mused. "It would have been a different story if they had stayed in the casa as they were ordered to do."

The canyon to the north was quiet. Patience hung on to Nathaniel, and couldn't let go. Her strength and her life just then seemed to depend on how closely she could hold him. The boy moodily kicked through the ruins, salvaging small things: a can, a tintype of the Hopes, a pot. And Charity, perhaps too young to comprehend the magnitude of her dangers, perked up and began to play in the dust, and then ran to the garden where there were crisp beans to eat right off the vine.

Augustin Talliferro peered through his spyglass at Jonathan poking through the rubble far below. He had seen it all from a vantage point on the eastern ridge. He had watched the cannon rumble up, and the gringa's flight to the strongpoint. He had watched the balls pulverize the casa—it was a show better than the cockfights in San Juan—and then he had seen the gringo hombres, harder now than before, shoot their way down the mountain.

He envied them their Winchesters that shot brass cartridges. They could fire almost as fast as a man could aim,
like the Henry Repeaters, and the magazines could hold
seventeen shells. What an hombre could do with a
weapon like that! His own cap and ball took twelve seconds to reload, even with much practice.

The technical difficulty was what troubled him now as
he watched the Hapgoods far below. It would take three
good shots to kill them, and he could brain the señorita
later. The muchacho, with the Winchester in hand as he
kicked through the rubble, would be easy. But the señor
and señora, only partly visible under the ledge, needed
only to drop to the ground to be safe there. He could not
reload fast enough to shoot them all at once. He wished
he were close in, where his pistola could bark.

But there was no point in hurrying. If there were double eagles in that rubble, the Hapgoods would find them
and dig them out. Let them collect the valuables. It
would save him work and assure that nothing was missed.
This was certainly the time to strike, while they were
defenseless, and when the wagon, and mules, and horses,
and cattle were all available. And when the Olivera
hombres were far away.

That Winchester the muchacho was carrying; that was
the key, he thought. He would have to slip close to the
muchacho and silently impale him with the blade. Then
he would have the Winchester.

"Jon," the señor called to the muchacho, "someone has
to bring down the horses, and you're elected. Now be
careful."

The boy trudged up the trail, rifle in hand, as Talliferro
watched from above. The young gringo was leaving. Perhaps he was going to fetch the caballos on the ridge
above. A quick, silent thrust and Talliferro would have
the weapon! And there would only be two left below, un-
aware.

Talliferro slithered back from the overlook and snaked his way north toward the head of the canyon where he could intercept the muchacho. The pale Majorcan was swift, and moved from rock to rock without a sound, like a stalking puma.

The untied horses, reins dangling, had drifted off the shoulder and down the trail that would take them to their familiar pasture and water. Jon found them a short way up from the head of the canyon. He boarded his sorrel, knowing that the baldface and Cotton would follow along.

Talliferro raced silently down into an arroyo that tumbled beside the trail, even as Jon and the horses, screened by mesquite, rode by. There would be no time for the knife; the muchacho was passing above, and in the saddle. Talliferro's mind raced even as he dashed nimbly along the arroyo behind the muchacho above. He wanted the Winchester. Had to have it! It would make him the terror of Mexico, he and the bandidos he'd gather around him!

He drew la pistola then, aimed at the retreating back, and let it bark. Jon had heard the last racing steps of the hombre and had started to turn when he felt a wicked blow strike his right chest, and then a flood of wetness and weakness. He lifted the Winchester dizzily with his left hand, saw the man behind, and fired. Then he grabbed the saddle horn with a death grip while consciousness dribbled out of him, and the sorrel bolted down the trail.

Jonathan's bullet furrowed across the back of Talliferro's pistol hand, breaking one bone, severing all the tendons that worked the fingers, and cutting the big artery. Talliferro's pistol dropped from numb fingers and then pain exploded in his head and his hand turned red. He cursed, and picked up la pistola with his good hand.

He was marked! For the first time in his life! Ayah, he had been reckless! He who was never reckless!

He stripped off his camisa and wrapped it around the pulpy hand to stanch the blood, and then stumbled back to the piñon grove where he had tied the mare. Each step shot a bolt of pain up his arm. His weakness alarmed him. He couldn't shoot!

The boy hung on as the horse clattered down upon the meadow. Pain and nausea washed over him, and his fingers finally released the Winchester near the rubble. Blood bubbled down his back from a hole below his shoulder blade, and from his chest, where there was a hole under his collarbone.

They had heard the shots, and now as the boy appeared, reeling on his horse, with half his torso bathed in glistening red, Nathaniel raced up to catch him as he sank off the horse, and carried him to the little stronghold and gently laid him out upon the sand.

"Oh no, no, no, no," Patience whispered as she found water and began to cleanse the wounds. "No, God, no." She wrapped his whole chest with her petticoat and knotted it as tightly as she could. Nathaniel found a blanket in the rubble, and wrapped Jon in it. The boy slipped into a deep coma, and what little breath they detected was ragged and feeble.

She had done what she could for his body, so she enclosed her son's face gently in her hands and prayed. The words stumbled and tripped in her mind, but it was prayer anyway, a prayer with a healing force that exuded from her fingertips and into the ashen face of the comatose youth.

Nathaniel tried to pray, too, but he couldn't. Instead, his burning eyes watched every rock, every leaf, every log, and every shadow, ready to blast anything that moved.

CHAPTER 11

"Ap-Good. Señor Ap-Good." The reedy voice rose out of the darkness from the ledge straight above Nathaniel, and lifted the hairs on his neck.

"Apgood. *No fuego.* Night Hawk. I come."

Relieved, Nathaniel welcomed the old shaman.

They had not dared to light a fire. And Nathaniel hadn't slept. In fact he felt too mean to sleep. He and Patience had shared their vigil through the long hours, listening to Jon's rasping breath. It had become uneven, and recently she discovered he was burning up with fever. She held his sweaty hand and wiped his face, and prayed helplessly.

The ghostly figure of the shaman materialized in the starlight and he kneeled beside the boy, listening.

"Spirits on the mountain send. Coyote say, go help. Good Papago medicine."

The ancient one untied the dressings and then pressed a poultice of something that looked like moss to the wounds. He poured an aromatic powder over the poultices, and wrapped Jon in a coarse clean fabric that materialized from somewhere on his wizened person. Still kneeling, he began a soft guttural song, as sad and lonely as the cry of a night hawk at midnight. It made Patience shiver and remember the fragility of flesh.

Nathaniel glared red-eyed into the night, and at the shaman, and out upon the murky mountain. He didn't like it. But Patience did, and she slipped her hand into his and squeezed a message to him. He sighed and settled back to await a black dawn.

Night Hawk finished his song at last and sat back. "*Gran Dios*—Brother Pierre. Him help," he said.

Nathaniel wondered what ideas and beliefs the old shaman and the monk had shared or debated.

"*La mañana. Hablo.* Brother Pierre," the Indian added.

He would see the monk in the morning, Nathaniel thought. And tell the monk of the sadness here. For some reason, that was comforting.

"*Bueno. Muy bueno.*" Nathaniel smiled.

The shaman rose, placed a thin hard hand over those of Patience and Nathaniel, and then vanished into the dark.

The boy seemed worse, and Patience began to dread the next minutes when the rasping would stop. Jon had reached some sort of crisis in the depths of his body.

Nathaniel impulsively kneeled beside his son as the youth thrashed and coughed. He put Jon's clammy hand between his own warm ones, and pressed.

"Jon! Jon! I know you can hear me. Listen! You're going to get well, boy. Lots of life ahead of you. You're just getting started, Jon. You're tougher than you think. Young. Strong. All muscled up out here. You're as much a man as I could want beside me. Get ahold, boy!"

Something quiet entered into the boy's breathing.

"I'm going to pray, Jon. And you do, too. Down in your head. Believe in it, Jon. You listen now. . . ."

Patience lifted Charity's head to her lap and listened to Nathaniel talk life into her failing son, talk him into hanging on, talking and talking. She stroked Charity's hair. The poor girl hadn't eaten—none of them had—and she slept fitfully.

Soon after the first gray light the boy's breathing smoothed and came regularly. His brow cooled and the hot flush left his cheeks. Patience's spirits lifted a bit. As the first rays of sun lit the top of the canyon, they knew he had weathered the worst.

It was time to get on with living, even though they dreaded ambush or whatever Ignacio Olivera had in store for them. They were starved. Patience picked up the Colt and began gathering whatever she could find in the rubble: beans, beets, carrots, salt. She found some utensils, and pulled onions from the garden. It would be enough.

Nathaniel unsaddled the horses. He had never left Jon's side during the night, and now he turned the animals into the pasture. Some reins were broken from the night's neglect, and these he set aside for repair. He built a crude stove for Patience out of adobe rubble, and built her a fire.

Then, while they waited for the vegetables to boil, the man and woman began sadly to gather what they could from the heaps of adobe and the dust and the fallen vigas. She found a cup and a precious knife. He painfully gathered dried pinto beans that had burst from a sack. She found the old Hapgood Bible, beneath some bricks, blown in two. She silently showed the two pieces to Nathaniel, and he set them carefully aside.

She found many of her clothes, unharmed in a trunk. He recovered four hundred cartridges and gratefully set them in the stronghold. She found some candles and a pillow, while he unearthed a bag of flour and a broken kerosene lantern. Charity found two forks and a scorpion, which Nathaniel killed for her.

Then they ate, and all three devoured seconds and thirds, until the pot was empty. Patience immediately started a new pot, using the pinto beans and more vegetables.

The rains would come soon, Nathaniel thought. The small shed near the corrals was intact. It was nothing but a square adobe, barely ten feet by ten inside. And there was no door—only the doorframe, because there had been no time to build one. There was some hay inside, and harness and implements. At least it was a refuge, and warmth for Jon.

Nathaniel hung a tarpaulin over the doorframe, and then forked the remaining hay flat along one wall for beds for them all. He hauled the harness out and brought their few pitiful possessions in. He punched some loopholes in the windowless walls, for protection.

Then he saddled Cotton, dropped his reata over the tongue of the wagon, and dragged it across the doorframe, but a little out. It would stop bullets and enable them to duck out safely under siege.

He found a usable chair in the rubble. The kitchen table lacked a leg but he dragged it to the shed and piled blocks under the missing corner. He brought the Winchesters and some of the ammunition to the shed, leaving the other weapons at the stronghold. By midafternoon they were resettled after a fashion, and Nathaniel began to mend reins and hammer at pots.

They hovered over Jonathan. His breath was regular but his eyes stayed shut and his face was gray. The mossy material had somehow drawn off the inflammation. Patience wanted to change the dressing, but hesitated, and decided to let well enough alone.

That evening Nathaniel gently carried the boy from the stronghold to the soft hay of the shed. The troubled look returned to Patience's eyes, but the trip was successful and the bleeding did not resume. As Nathaniel lowered his son into the hay, the boy's eyes opened. Love passed between them for a moment, and then the boy's eyes closed again.

"Praise God," Nathaniel said as he stood up.

They were settled somehow. The day had been quiet, and they had needed that quiet. Patience milked Jezebel and turned her out for the night.

Jonathan's eyes opened again.

"Thirsty," he whispered, and Patience quickly lifted his head and ladled warm broth into his mouth. He swallowed it all, and Patience ran her hand through his long hair. He smiled wanly.

"I'll kill the son of a bitch," he said suddenly, and Patience dropped the ladle.

"Even-steven," he said, looking squarely at his mother, and she slowly remembered a reckless moment in the past.

Nathaniel smiled disapprovingly.

Jon settled back to sleep in the hay, and Charity curled up beside him. There were no windows, and Nathaniel and Patience found themselves eager for open air.

He unfastened the wagon tailgate and let it drop, so they could both sit on the wagon bed and enjoy the twilight view down the dusky canyon. He set down the rifle that had been at hand all day, and let the tension seep out of him at last.

She brought up the subject they had avoided for hours.

"There are good surgeons in Boston," she said quietly. "When he's better we can take him there."

". . . and stay?"

"Yes."

"I thought you'd be notioning that way."

"I don't have to tell you why," she replied.

"Hate to give this place up."

"I'll miss it too, Nathaniel. But I want us alive, and I'm tired of being afraid every minute, every hour."

He sighed.

"I've got some business to attend to, and then maybe we'll go."

"What business? Your business will get you killed," she said bitterly. "I want you alive. I want"—she turned to him and pressed a hand over his—"more beautiful nights. . . ."

Memories quieted them both for a minute.

"I have to do it, Patience," he said at last.

"Make me a widow. You against the whole lot of them, Nathaniel Hapgood!" she snapped bitterly. "How can I argue with you? You're going to do something, and nothing I say matters."

"You don't even know what I'm thinking of. Aren't you jumping the gun a bit?" he asked edgily.

She didn't speak.

"I'm going to sleep," she said moodily, and disappeared through the dark doorway.

He sat alone, thinking, doubting.

Maybe we should go back. Be a little tame after this. But safe. I could sell the herd easily. . . . But damned if I'll run off with my tail between my legs like that. No. I couldn't live with myself if I saw a coward in the mirror. And maybe I can make us safe here, after all. . . .

He knocked the wood planking of the old freight wagon affectionately.

"Always knew this big buggy would come in handy when I really needed it," he said aloud.

~~~~~

The hand throbbed viciously, and each throb shot a wave of pain up Talliferro's arm and into his skull. So great was the pain that he couldn't think, and not being able to think was for him a deprivation.

His camisa, wrapped bulkily around the hand, turned red and then brown in the sun. He had lost much blood and was lightheaded. With his good hand he lifted the canteen and drained it.

He stumbled back along the ridge, worried that more shots might ring out. It was the first time that he, the hunter, had become the hunted. He cursed savagely at his impetuosity: never before had he acted impulsively, and that was why he lived while lesser practitioners of his trade died against the wall, or had hands lopped off.

He had to get back to the hacienda, where Ignacio kept an up-to-date pharmacopoeia. But he couldn't travel without a camisa in the June sun. His pale flesh would roast in an hour.

The mare was tied in a juniper grove nearby. Perhaps he could lay low in the shade there, until *el sol* would let him travel. He needed time to think. His mind wasn't functioning.

He slithered up the last rocky slope with only the thought of reaching the mare in mind. He heard the rattle and leaped wildly sideways as the snake struck, and he tumbled into sharp rock. The snake missed but now his elbow was skinned and his knee hurt, and his pain turned to rage. He found the mare in the shade, and kicked her sideways, into the glare so he'd have a cool place to protect his skin.

Why go back to the hacienda at all? There was nothing there except more dirty work for Ignacio. He had some clothing, a few reales, and an old pistola in a trunk, and it pained him to abandon them. But they were nothing— mere trinkets—compared to the Hapgood cattle and wagon and wealth.

They wouldn't even miss him. He lived a solitary life in his own casita and was often gone for days. It would be weeks before they realized—and by then he'd be a wealthy man on the camino to Guadalajara or Vera Cruz.

But just now he needed to protect his pasty white

body. His mind was functioning again. Of course! He had the solution before his eyes, on the back of the *yegua*. The saddle blanket, made from wool sheared from hacienda sheep. Many a time on the trails Talliferro had been chilled and had used the blankets as serapes.

With his good hand he loosened the latigo until the cinch hung loose. He tugged the blanket. The mare skittered sideways, unused to such clumsiness. He booted her in the belly.

He tugged the folded blanket again, and this time it fell to the ground. He drew the cinch tight again so he'd be ready to travel immediately. Such caution was how he stayed alive, he thought, proud of himself. Then he drew his throwing knife and sawed a slit into the blanket, and pulled the makeshift poncho over his head. He was pleased. Intelligence was the key!

He mounted clumsily, with his bad hand screaming. But the mare stood quietly, making it easy. She was a good mare, powerful, sound, obedient. Ignacio would miss her—he knew every one of his scores of horses. Talliferro smiled grimly. El patrón could afford the loss. In time, Talliferro would have the Hapgood horses, too, and a fine remuda like that would ensure his safety and command a price.

Painfully, he tied the reins together so he could drop them over the withers without losing them, to shoot or drink. There was nothing but silence there on the ridge, so he spurred the mare into a soft walk and pointed her north toward the great blue mountain.

He found the trail rising up the west flank, the trail that led to the towering blue rock where he had watched the Hapgood muchacho. There would surely be a cave or sheltered ledge behind, and water. It was obviously defensible: one man could fend off an army picking its way up that talus. Best of all, it would keep him close to the

Hapgoods while his hand mended. They would not be escaping with his cattle and wagon and mules.

He spotted the great slab of rock and worked the mare up the steep slope to it. Nausea wrenched him and he needed a shelter badly now. The cave was there, and he was delighted. In its murk he saw barrels of provisions, and at the rear a pool of black water. He led the uneasy mare in to drink, and filled his dry canteen, and then began to rummage through the barrels with his good hand.

It amused him to think that the Hapgoods were provisioning him. He found no weapons, and that disappointed him, but there was some powder. There was some carefully wrapped jerky, salt, flour, and other staples. He found an old camisa that fit, some pantalones, and a sombrero. There were rawhide and rags to dress his wound. There were even some spare blankets, and these he piled into a soft bed, for he was too tired to think.

He released the mare on the grass below, and lowered himself luxuriously into the blankets. His hand didn't hurt so much.

He slept fitfully. He had a fever and a headache. And in the night he was awakened suddenly. But it was nothing. A white flash outside, and the distant boom of thunder. Well, why not? San Juan's Day would soon be here, and the rains always came about then. So, it was nothing. Nothing.

CHAPTER 12

The next day Jonathan awakened now and then, but he coughed up blood and black material that alarmed Patience.

Nathaniel considered the desperate weakness of his son and decided that for the next days there was no option but to stay in the canyon. If trouble came, he would surrender at once. He doubted that even those tough pistoleros would kill in cold blood.

His afternoon's task was the construction of a pack saddle, which was essential to the plan that was forming in his mind. He adapted a riding saddle to the task, using old harness, rawhide, and salvaged boards. By late afternoon he had a crude saddle, laced together with liberal amounts of rawhide thong.

It was designed to fit the off-side lead mule, the one with the notched ear, whose name was General Sherman. Nathaniel took his time with the saddle: it would have to support heavy weight, without failure, at a critical moment. Patience watched his progress quizzically, but said nothing.

Jon awoke and smiled at his parents.

"I know who it was," he said softly. "Got a good look at him and that smoking pistol of his. The one with the big forehead. No mistake. I'd know that"—he censored himself—"man anywhere."

So it was the Evil One, Nathaniel thought. The strange, pale one that had made him so queasy. The one Night Hawk says stalks these mountains bringing terror to the Papagoes.

When the mules came to water, Nathaniel penned them and looked them over. They hadn't been used for months, and had obviously prospered. He respected them. He had a theory that they were twice as smart as horses, and their intelligence was precisely why they were harder to catch and less tractable. The dumb horses had always succumbed to his will sooner or later, but these blasted mules stayed ornery and wily.

He cut out General Sherman and cornered him. The big mule was all set to bolt, but the man sweet-talked the mule until he was able to scratch his jaw and slip a halter over his head. He wanted General Sherman to experience the packsaddle, and weight on his back.

After General Sherman was rigged up, Nathaniel walked him awhile and then tied heavy mesquite logs to the packsaddle. It was a new experience for the mule, who liked neither the weight nor the separation from muledom. But the more Nathaniel worked, the more resigned the beast was. The last thing the man wanted was a balky mule for the mission he had in mind.

Patience built a picnic table from some shutters and blocks she salvaged, and then added two benches. She served supper outside, a marvelous repast, considering what little food there was.

They ate greedily, and sat back, each in his private reverie. There had been a barrier between them since the previous night, and now the talk and the usual sharing of the day didn't come. She couldn't understand him.

Her hopes were simple: when Jon was better they

would carry him in the freight wagon to Tucson, along
with whatever they could salvage; sell the herd, and go
back to Concord and start over.

He knew that her hopes were not far from his, but he
had some business to settle first, business he had been
mulling all day. He had shut her out of it.

"Allo, allo, Monsieur Hapgood." The trumpet voice
rolled down from high up the trail.

"Brother Pierre! Come on down! Welcome," Nathaniel
called back, pleased.

Soon a brown cassock materialized in the twilight, and
then the frail form of Night Hawk, and behind, two Papago boys leading a burdened burro.

"How goes Jonathan?" the monk asked directly.

"Worst of it's over, I guess. But he's coughing blood
and weak as a pup. He could get a fever again. We worry
plenty," Nathaniel responded.

"May I see him?" The monk paused, choosing his
words. "I believe my prayers will help. Sometimes . . .
I've been an instrument of healing. I've felt—power.
Flowing out of my hands when I've touched a sick person. Monsieur Hapgood, I'd like to be with the boy a minute, but—" he added circumspectly, "only with your permission."

"By all means," Nathaniel responded.

"Good! We'll hear all the news later. But I can't rest
until I have seen Jonathan for a minute or two."

The cassock swirled through the canvas door. Patience
looked at Nathaniel and smiled for the first time that day,
and then she surveyed the shaman and the two youths
who stood mutely before the pile of rubble.

"You must be very hungry. I'll have something for you
in a little bit," she said to them.

He looked at her, and the table, and barked a command
to the black-haired boys. They unloaded a feast from the

baskets on the burro: venison, peppers, pinto beans, cactus fruit, corn meal. In a few moments they had spread a cold meal. Night Hawk ate a little; the Indian boys a great deal. And they all waited for the monk to emerge from the dark shed.

"The boy rests quietly," was all he said, but the soft brown eyes found Nathaniel's and were full of kindness and peace. Nathaniel felt strangely reassured, and Patience knew within herself that some great force had touched her son.

He ate sparingly while Nathaniel described the events of the last days. Patience added very little; she remembered almost nothing. The friar translated for Night Hawk and the youths seemed to understand.

"Night Hawk and I have a question. Do you own a black horse?" the Franciscan asked.

"No, never have," Nathaniel replied.

"We saw one on the western shoulder of Baboquivari. Below the cave."

Nathaniel absorbed the news silently.

"Tell Night Hawk that Jon was shot by the one he calls the Gourd Head, the Evil One. The boy saw him," Nathaniel said softly.

Night Hawk nodded; he needed no translation. Then the shaman spoke at length to the friar.

"He knew who was there when we passed below. He says he can smell death, and the Evil One smells of death. He kept the knowledge to himself to avoid alarming the rest of us."

They talked long into the evening, diverse people bonded by trouble and fear, as well as friendship. Then the boys bedded down at the stronghold; the friar made himself comfortable in the wagon bed, and Night Hawk slipped into the dark toward places known only to himself.

In the jet black of the shed, with the sweet scent of hay in his nostrils and the children slumbering, Nathaniel reached over to kiss Patience. But she had withdrawn far inside herself. She accepted the kiss passively, though a part of her yearned to reach out across the void to him. Then he rolled over on his back and stared into the gloom.

At first light he began harnessing the mules, and by the time the rest were stirring he had the team rigged and waiting. He realized that the friar had been standing at the corral, pensively, watching him.

"I'm going to Tucson and—around," Nathaniel said edgily. "I sure appreciate your help and hope you'll stay on. . . ."

The friar caught a tone of voice that he hadn't heard before, so he nodded quietly and waited. Patience did her best to scare up a good breakfast, but they ate silently with the dour Nathaniel imposing a mood on them all. Night Hawk had vanished, and the Indian boys were silent.

It was time to go. Nathaniel rose abruptly and caught Patience's eye. He tried to say something but couldn't. There was hurt and worry in her face. He turned, exchanged a troubled glance with the friar, and stalked away. When the wagon was loaded with a few supplies, he jumped up to the boot and hawed the team down the canyon, not looking back.

Patience wanted to lecture him, make him stop whatever he was doing. She tried to compose herself, but only wept. Brother Pierre sighed, and inside himself asked his Lord for the means to protect this desperate little family.

Nathaniel drew up at Newmeyer's Mining Supply and Assay Office, out a way on the camino del norte. He leaped down, stretched, and wound his way through piles of picks, wheelbarrows, shoring timbers, light rail, barrels of spikes, and ore cars, until he spotted a graying man in a leather apron adding columns.

"Have any blasting powder?" Nathaniel asked.

"Sure. How much you want?"

"How about thirty barrels?" Nathaniel asked.

"Ain't got anywhere near that," the man replied quietly. "Let's see. There's nineteen out there. We keep it in a bunker up near the Rillito River."

"Where can I get more?" Nathaniel demanded.

"Mister, I just don't know for sure. Likely some in the mining camps."

"I don't have time for that," Nathaniel snapped. "I'll take all of yours."

Newmeyer eyed him curiously.

"Fixing to do some mining?"

"You might call it that," said Nathaniel darkly.

"What kind of ore? Maybe I can help a bit—"

"Mining water," Nathaniel rasped. He had started to feel ornery.

"Oh, well, we sometimes sell a little powder to people building ditches. They often hit rock. That's the future of Arizona, irrigation."

"My ditch is already dug," said Nathaniel obscurely. "Now let's have a price on those nineteen."

Newmeyer studied the list. "Eleven dollars a barrel gold, or thirteen greenback. Hundred twenty-five pounds a barrel, average. Mister, you must be planning to blow a hell of a hole."

"Anything special I should know about hauling it?"

"Naw. Just don't hit no potholes." The proprietor grinned.

"I'll pay now and pick them up at the bunker. Give me plenty of fuse," he added.

"Mister, you're going to need plenty of fuse," Newmeyer retorted as Nathaniel stalked out.

Four hours and one fiery Mexican meal later, Nathaniel Hapgood was cautiously steering the freight wagon, laden with nineteen barrels of blasting powder, up the slope of the Ajo Road. The air was moist with an easterly breeze, and there were great cumulous clouds above. He saw some lightning over Baboquivari that twenty-third day of June. The late afternoon was ferociously hot, and Nathaniel yearned for those lowering clouds to deluge him and his caked mules. But he knew if they did, the arroyos would run, his powder might be soaked if any staves weren't tight, and he would be delayed for days. So he flipped the long reins to give General Sherman the word, and rumbled south until sundown.

The mules were restless and so was Nathaniel. They smelled water in the moist wind, and milled around through the night. Nathaniel built no fire, and unrolled his bed some distance from the wagon, full of foreboding. He was on a doomsday trip, and he wondered whether he'd ever see Patience again.

There were few stars, and he knew heavy clouds were boiling across a tensioned sky. It was preternaturally quiet, as if the whole life of the desert was awaiting the first explosions of summer thunder, and the racing, life-giving rains. There had been none; only a few fickle clouds and some mendacious thunder around Baboquivari.

San Juan's Day dawned gray, although the sun appeared from time to time amid towering clouds that made the plate of the earth seem infinitesimal. The black-bottomed clouds boiled ominously out of the east and each bank of them seemed darker than the previous one. Nathaniel hadn't slept well, and the weather made him owly.

He rode boldly south down the Altar Valley, cradling his carbine in his lap while his big hands gripped fistfuls of reins. Whirlwinds and dust devils whipped through the team and danced away, and with them sand and alkali dust dug into his eyes and the eyes of his mules. He squinted and spat.

By three, he was some two miles north of the Hacienda del Leon. There were gray rain clouds spitting across the east, and thunder racketing across the heavens. He sweated one moment only to be chilled the next by some icy downdraft from some unfathomable height above. A forked bolt struck ahead, not far from the hacienda, and boomed back on Nathaniel.

He abandoned the wagon road. Darkness lowered suddenly and drops splattered the dust and smacked his face. He eased carefully through rocky topland and then drew up on a ridge north of the dam, and gazed down on the long sliver of water, rippling gray. He snapped a signal to General Sherman, and the big mule began to lead the team down a slope of ragged rock. The fateful barrels skittered and clattered behind him as the iron tires crunched through rocky rubble. Fifty yards from the dam, with a steep arroyo blocking his path, Nathaniel called a halt.

The spitting rain turned to drizzle, and the thunder boomed louder. Sweating even in the whipping breezes, Nathaniel unhooked General Sherman and cinched up the packsaddle. Then he dropped the tailgate and coaxed the first bulky barrel into his arms, and lashed it to the saddle. Then he staggered with the second barrel to the far side of the mule, and lashed it in place. He led General Sherman down through raw rock, which the rain had made treacherous, to the foot of the moss-blackened dam. He was alone.

He found an arm of rock projecting alongside the south

façade of the dam, and wedged the barrels between it and the wall. Then he led the mule up to the wagon. His shirt was drenched, as much from sweat and fear as from rain. He eased the third and fourth barrels into place as lightning flickered overhead, and thunder drummed incessantly.

He felt shaky, already winded, so he paused for breath and let the mule drink. He hadn't realized he would get so tired so fast. He had the eerie feeling that someone was staring at him, and he whirled around. No one. Slate-gray rain. Reluctantly he turned back to the dam, and felt those same sad eyes penetrating him. Eyes like Patience's, but not hers; eyes that haunted him.

He turned feverishly to his task and carted four more barrels down the slick slope. One wet barrel slipped from his fingers and cracked sickeningly into a rock, and his heart thudded wildly for minutes after. Eight barrels.

He wiped his wet face and rested again, sticky and sandy. Again the sad, knowing eyes bored into him, and this time he remembered Don Ignacio telling him, at the niche of the Virgen de Guadalupe, that she was protectress of the dam. He stalked over to the niche. The image was there, small, serene, and surrounded by a sunburst of gold leaf. A statue, lifeless, painted, a beatific smile on wooden lips, and no sadness in her eyes. But he felt those sad eyes on him once again as he plunged back to business.

The rains came in heavy gusts and lightning rippled across the abysses above while Nathaniel wrestled the next four barrels to the dam. Then he collapsed into sloppy sand, too weary to move, and watched the water trickle over the lip twenty feet above. The trickle widened, and he realized the arroyo was running and the lake above was full. In minutes a great flood would roar over the top of the dam and wash his barrels away—and all his plans.

He raced General Sherman back to the wagon and hitched him. He yanked fuse from the boot, and a handful of lucifers, and skidded down to the wet barrels.

He sliced the fuse in half, not trusting just one in this downpour. He jammed them into the bungs of two lower barrels, forcing himself to take time and do things right. He grew calmer. He had visualized this very scene countless times in the last few days. He pinned the fuses down with loose rock and kept them above the muck.

He paused a moment and there came to him the sound of Patience screaming, distant as an eagle's cry. Now he wanted to make her safe. Nathaniel's sudden reverie was snapped by the mounting flood of water over the dam. He huddled over the longer fuse, cupped it in the wind, and scratched three of the lucifers. A blinding bolt struck that very instant with a simultaneous blast that battered his ears, and he jerked back and fell in the slop. Shaking, he lit three more and this time saw the fuse sputter into vicious life. He jammed the lit fuse into the end of the unlit one until they both spat at the universe.

Then he walked purposefully—no sense falling in the wet rock—up and out of the arroyo, to his wagon, and boarded with an enforced calm that belied the turmoil boiling inside him.

"Haw," he yelled into the wind, and cracked the long whip down on the mules. The wagon creaked away and then banged through puddled rock. When he had gone a hundred yards, the world turned orange. A vast light rose up behind him, illuminating the undersides of the black clouds for miles. The rain glistened orange as it fell, and the eerie light glittered off rock and cactus and his own wet hands in the purple of the day. There were three distinct whooms, and three pulses of warm air that shot through cold breezes. And then a mounting roar that crescendoed louder than the storm.

Nathaniel whanged his whip, and the mules danced. He feared there would be boiling arroyos ahead to trap him. He steered restlessly, wheeling the team between boulders and through mesquite. He just missed a rounded rock, and bounced across a field of yucca. The unused barrels of powder danced behind him and clattered back until one by one they tumbled into the sandy muck of the desert. He turned his team into the bottoms, with holly bushes near the road, and raced ahead. The wagon lurched and the last of the barrels rolled under a desert holly just before he rolled out on the firm road.*

* Two years later a lone-riding cowboy was passing through that country on his way to Nogales. He spotted a buck at a place exactly where Nathaniel had driven the wagon wildly through the storm, spilling the powder barrels. For two years the sun and rain had beaten on the barrel that had rolled under the holly bush, but most of the powder was as potent as ever.

The cowboy, a red-headed giant known in all the bunkhouses of Arizona as a notorious braggart and teller of tall tales, decided to have some venison as long as the buck was just parking there. So he eased his carbine out and lined up a nice shot. What he didn't know was that the old barrel of powder was directly behind the buck.

He shot and the buck blew up. In fact, that buck sent up a geyser of rock, a flash thirty yards high, and knocked him clear out of his saddle. The spooked horse took off at a gallop.

The cowboy, a bit dazed, got up, dusted off his chaps, and eyed the five-foot crater where the buck had been.

"That old buck musta been full of bad meat," he said to himself. "Glad I didn't take a bite or he'd a blown me teeth out."

He collected his randy horse and began to realize that *now* he had a tale to tell the boys, and gospel truth, too. As he rode, he began to work up his yarn, because it would take telling.

"I shot me a buck tuther day that plumb blew up and knocked me clean off my bronc."

He mulled that a little and didn't like it. No one would ever believe it. So he tried another tack.

"Do you fellers know what sort of meat 'tis that blows up? I shot me a buck tuther day . . ."

That angle didn't sound so good, either. He worried the tale around for three days and never could come up with a version he could tell. By the time he got to Nogales he was a changed man. Never quite himself, they said of him after. And the story was, he took to religion and was never seen again in the cow camps.

Twice he was forced to halt at a running arroyo, even after the storm had passed west. His own tracks had washed out instantly, leaving no trace. He turned frequently, and saw no one behind. He wiped water from his carbine and continued north through a drenched universe, soaked, cold, troubled, and relieved. Now they could live here without fear.

CHAPTER 13

The explosion blew a hole nearly twenty feet across at the base of the dam, which narrowed down to ten feet at the top. It was not enough to send a wall of water rolling down on the hacienda, but enough to loose a tide several feet high upon the delta where the casitas and outbuildings stood.

Moments after the strange orange flash had died away, the families of the great hacienda began to hear a rumbling so deep it sounded as if the earth itself were splitting in two.

The rolling water reached the corrals first. They were lowest and closest to the arroyo bed. The racing water ripped through the mesquite poles and forced horses and burros to face the tide. The water rose rapidly and one by one the fence poles popped out of the earth as if a giant derrick had plucked them. They released a mass of mesquite wood that formed the corral walls. The debris slammed into the animals, knocking them over. By the time the water reached their hocks they could no longer resist, and were swept downstream, neighing and bellowing and whinnying. Some were deposited on a gentle bank nearby, but most were carried far into Mexico.

The water boiled through adobe sheds, dissolving mud mortar and hammering blocks free until buildings collapsed. The torrent carried off saddles, bridles, harness, lumber, hay, whips, grain, carriages, tools, rope, a grist mill, salt, and hides. Far below, a mile into Mexico, many of these items were deposited on sandy beaches.

Manuel Arrosca was frightened. His casita shook and he could see only boiling water from his window. And then the water seemed to rise from the very walls and floor.

"Come, Rosa! Bring the niño!" he cried, pausing to stuff his rosary into his pantalones. They struggled through the knee-high stream toward higher ground where the great casa and chapel were, and finally stumbled, exhausted, into the chapel, where even in the storm the candles burned quietly before the great image of the Virgin.

Capitán Pedro Castillo-Armas occupied a fine villa on a hillside above the great casa, a home befitting one of his rank. It had real glass, and the windows gave him a splendid view to the west, toward Presumido Peak. He had been drawn to those windows a moment earlier by an unearthly orange light that glowed off the thunderheads. Sharp jarring rattled the panes. In an instant the veteran officer understood. Twenty or thirty vaqueros and their little ones were in mortal danger. He rushed to the plaza, which was even then inundated.

He found Lupe and Natividad trapped in their casita in three feet of water, and he carried the ancient woman to safety while the old man clung to him in the tide. He saw a boy, the maid Juanita's son, half drowned, clinging to a mesquite limb, and he hauled the boy to higher ground. He broke into three more casitas and gathered terrified families into a human chain with locked hands, which enabled the strong to pull the weak through the floodtide.

Help came now from the tough vaqueros, and he directed them toward each casita. The bronzed men found women and children and dragged them through waist-high currents to safe ground or, in some cases, safe tree limbs.

When the storm first broke, Ignacio Olivera did exactly as he always did when the rains came: he closeted himself in his bedroom where there was a small altar. There, behind three-foot adobe walls that muffled the raging weather, he thanked God, and especially San Juan, whose feast day this was, for the rains that gave life to his hacienda. And thus he missed the strange orange flash, the roar, the concussions, and the rising flood for some minutes. The waters came close to the casa and then receded.

After his devotions, Don Ignacio looked out of his window upon a scene of incredible devastation. He saw his own tough hombres straining through boiling waters, pulling people from their melting casitas, dragging them to the chapel. He ran swiftly to his study, where he kept three fine reatas, masterpieces of Mexican leatherwork, and threw them to his vaqueros.

The braided ropes were instantly useful. The vaqueros built loops and whirled them to stranded compadres. At one point three people grabbed a floating loop and two vaqueros slowly pulled them to low water. Gradually a soaked crowd gathered in the chapel. Some wept; many prayed, shivering in the dark, cold afternoon. All were homeless. The water had ripped away all they possessed. One by one they straggled in, safe and alive, as the water receded. Ignacio and the capitán counted heads. After twenty minutes everyone was accounted for—save one.

"God reached out and struck him down," Ignacio sighed, wondering at the bottom of his soul whether the blame was all Talliferro's. "There's nothing left of him. No casita, no possessions—and no body. Perhaps they will find it in Mexico when the vultures tell us where to look."

Augustin Talliferro's small house had indeed disappeared. Later they found the dun horse alive, and the discovery assured them that the pale hombre had drowned at the hacienda. Among the missing horses, however, was a choice black mare.

Maria Olivera pitied the sixty-odd shivering, homeless people whose work and lives had revolved around the Hacienda del Leon. She emptied the closets of clothing and carried it all to her little ones. She gathered dry blankets and pillows and made the old and half-drowned comfortable.

She recruited a few women and set them to work in the vast kitchen of the casa. Feeding all those mouths was going to be a great enterprise in itself. Food stores had washed away, but beef could be slaughtered and milk would soon be available when the cows were gathered. She tromped through muck from casita to ruined casita recovering things for her people, even while the last of the rains soaked her.

But it was not the provision of material things that made the humble ones suddenly aware of the patrona.

"You had a great swim!" she laughed at the niños.

"Come to the chapel, mamacita, where you'll be safe and warm. Here's a pillow. Bring the cat now, and give thanks for life!"

"*Una santa*," whispered old Lupe, after Maria had tucked a blanket around her, and had found a pillow for old Natividad. She took the women to her own room, where they could change into dry clothing and hang the wet things around the fire.

Ignacio turned over the casa to the women, and toured his hacienda well before the water had drained off. It was a desolate sight. A three-foot-high sand bar snaked across the plaza. The heart of the ranch, the corrals and sheds, had vanished and now there was nothing but a drenched mudflat there. Even the anvil had disappeared. The ca-

sitas closest to the arroyo were gone, and the ones on
slightly higher ground were standing but ruined. The
flagpole stood, and the green and white and red banner
flapped wetly in the silence.

He saw cattle on the hills, hundreds of them. They
would soon be lacking water, he thought dourly. The sun
would bake the wet earth into cracked dry cake. He
would have to make decisions soon. There was good
water at the south ranch, Tres Arroyos, thirty miles into
Mexico. Twenty of his vaqueros were there now, and his
own casa there was always ready for him. It would be a
refuge; a place for his cattle and people. . . .

Ignacio grieved. Slowly, he trudged westward to the
dam, and saw the gaping hole in its south flank. Behind it
was a long canyon of mud. Water still roared through the
hole as the desert shook off the deluge and dumped it into
the arroyo beds far above. He absorbed the devastation
for several minutes and then stalked back to the casa, his
boots squishing water in the dusk.

He let himself into his study through the outside door
and then locked all the doors. He stared moodily into the
fire Juanita had built for him, there beneath the portraits
of Luz, his grandfather, his father and mother, and General Santa Anna.

Pedro Castillo-Armas was an experienced leader of
men, and as the water receded he organized detail parties
and sent them into the wet evening. He set one group to
cleaning the usable casitas and building fires in them. Another group he assigned to sanitation: all drinking water
was to be boiled, and the remaining outhouses limed. He
sent another part to salvage whatever was salvageable,
and start it drying. Still others were sent to hunt for horses
and burros and cows. A twosome was set to slaughtering
an aged cow so the hacienda would have meat. Boys were

sent to build simple corrals of driftwood and any other
material at hand.

By dusk he had achieved some semblance of order. The
hacienda had risen from the water like a wet bear, and
had shaken off the flood. Men returned with horses and
burros. Others brought milk cows, wet hens and roosters.
Casitas capable of sleeping about thirty people were readied. All had been fed from the great pot of beans and
chili on the refectory table in the great casa.

There had been a perfunctory prayer for the soul of
Augustin Talliferro, while the unwavering candle flames
glowed. The great room of the casa had been turned into
a dormitory for men, and the married had been given
bedrooms that opened on the gracious rear patio.

The capitán overlooked nothing: that night he posted
Gomez and Juanito on sentry duty. Each was to take a
two-hour horseback tour while the other rested in the
casa kitchen. If they discovered anyone lurking in the
June night, the capitán wanted him taken alive.

Pedro Castillo-Armas trudged up the hill to his villa
just in time to see the setting sun illumine the dark bellies
of the clouds in the west. Far to the north, the day's storm
hung blackly over Baboquivari. The capitán was soaked
and weary but unwilling to go to bed, so he sat at his
west windows watching the fading panorama. Dusk
came, and with it a timid knocking. He opened the door
to Maria, astonished. It was unthinkable for her to be
here.

"I wish to come in," she said at last.

"Of course," he replied, and she entered into his austere military rooms for the first time. He lit a lamp and
stirred the fire. It was Sonoran summer, but the night was
chill.

She stood beside the fire and he noticed that she was
soaked, and that the wet cotton was clinging to her young

figure. The firelight danced through the translucent wetness, silhouetting her whole body, and suddenly his heart was hammering.

"I came to thank you," she said softly. "Without you, many of our little ones would have died. And the whole hacienda would be . . . paralyzed."

"Señorita Maria, we must thank God it was not more serious," he replied gravely.

"Who would imagine the storm would break the dam?" she asked.

He paused, uncertain whether to say what he knew.

"Maria. The storm didn't collapse the dam."

She looked at him quizzically, waiting.

"The orange flash. The concussion. You didn't hear it or see it? It was a great explosion right in the middle of the storm. The dam was blown up."

"An hombre?"

"One or several." He sighed darkly. "There's only one hombre it could have been. An eye for an eye. That was his message to your father. A rancho for a hacienda . . ."

The firelight flickered translucently through the cotton of her blusa.

"Come away from the fire before you scorch yourself," he said tautly. But some awareness dawned within her, some exciting thought, and she smiled regally at him.

It was time for her to leave; time for him to usher her away, this twenty-four-year-old daughter of his patrón, a girl eighteen years younger than himself.

"Señorita, I am pleased that you came. I've meant to talk to you for some time. . . . I appreciate your sentiments about my labors of the afternoon," he said stiffly.

"But I'm not done talking yet," she replied with a recklessness that surprised herself. "I want to talk about Papa."

"Yes?"

"He's in his study. He's been there for hours with all the doors locked. Juanita tried to bring him food, but he sent her away. Pedro, what's he doing?"

"A man whose estate is half ruined in twenty minutes needs time to think and discipline his soul," said the capitán. "I would have done the same."

She turned to face the fire, and he wondered how long she intended to stay.

"I know what he's thinking," she said softly. "Pedro, we'll soon be Mexican citizens again. At Tres Arroyos. He's burying this—all of this in the norte—now. He's conducting his own private funeral in there."

"I doubt he'll just give all this up and leave," he ventured. "But in any case, two thirds of your land is in Mexico, including some of the best water."

"I'm ready to go. Tres Arroyos is a beautiful rancho," she said. "I'm lonely here in the norte. It's always been my home, but it has been my prison, too. I must live where my father lives," she added. "Pedro, it's your prison, too."

"Prison? I don't know what you're talking about."

His cold caution only provoked her daring.

"Why are you here on the frontera, so far from . . . people?"

"I choose to be!" he retorted.

"That's right! Here all alone, all alone with the Virgin!"

"Señorita, you are being sacrilegious." He drew himself up in a military posture and faced her.

"I'm not talking about Our Lady; I'm talking about you."

"It's been a hard day, and I'm tired."

"Some men—some men like you who have been to Spain—conceive a love for the Virgin, who is beautiful, always silent. Who never snaps or demands or scolds, and who always smiles serenely. And who never reaches out her arms to hold them. They love only the ideal; never the mortal woman."

She blushed hotly, not meaning to plunge so far.

"I'm sorry, Pedro. I also am tired, and maybe angry, and I said things I never intended to say."

But he was fascinated by what she said. Her words were ridiculous, and yet they had pierced him in some strange way.

"The Virgin is perfect and she is always beautiful," Maria added quietly. "I look at her image, and then I look at myself in my looking glass, and . . ."

Neither of them spoke for minutes. She resisted an impulse to leave, to flee down the slope to her casa and the safety of her room. But she was not in the mood to be safe.

He looked at her as she gazed into the red mesquite coals. Until tonight he had seen only those plain cheeks and somber face. But this evening he had seen more: first the silhouette of her fine figure, and now a fathomable dignity; a cant of her head that made her handsome, and liquid brown eyes that were full of wisdom and suppressed passion. He saw a maturity that had ripened out of long suffering, and an eagerness to love that sprang from a lifetime of loneliness.

She turned to face him, expectantly. In all her life she had never been kissed. And now the beat of his heart and the power of his arms released feelings she had never known.

Long before the rest of the hacienda was stirring, Don Ignacio was out prowling. He walked to the dam and observed the curious hole. For the first time in his life the leonine man was weary in his soul. He had been tired countless times, but never weary like this. He had not

seen or heard the blast, but his practiced eye told him the
ragged hole was not caused by structural failure. An eye
for an eye, he remembered, and not even his antagonism
allayed the curious sympathy he felt for the Norte Americano. But of course they would die for this. All of them.
No one could inflict such a blow on the house of Olivera
and expect to live.

He splashed through the wide arroyo and walked along
its south bank, pausing to look at the flats below where a
dozen fine mesquite pens had contained fine animals the
day before. From the hill where he stood he could see the
course of the water: if the explosion had been much
larger the water would have flooded the casa itself. He almost wished it had. If he had been alerted soon enough,
he would have sent a party out to destroy Hapgood.

He turned away from the stricken hacienda and walked
south, up a gentle slope to the sacred ground. The graves
of his grandparents were here; his parents; his uncles and
aunts; two brothers; several infants, and—he stopped
painfully at the ornate grillwork that protected the grave
of his own Luz.

Years before, the surveyors with the International
Boundary Commission had brought him here and had
shown him where the border ran. It shocked him deeply.
Now, almost two decades later, he could scarcely remember the line. There was a milepost somewhere to the
east. He knew only that his hacienda was on the wrong
side, and that the pernicious line ran somewhere near,
perhaps through this very cemetery.

He sat beside Luz's grave, remembering as he always
did the love, happy chatter, and regal dignity of his bride.
It would be hard to leave these graves behind, in an alien
land. Harder than abandoning the whole northern third
of the Olivera grant. How close these graves were to their
homeland! But now these spirits were doomed to an eter-

nity in an alien place. He would be buried here too, beside Luz, in this land not of his choosing. And people who spoke the difficult English tongue would come here and not care.

"Ah, Luz," he sighed. "This is the hardest part. At Tres Arroyos you'll be far away. I won't be able to come here often, as I always have. Who'll bring you flowers and keep the candle lit? Someday I'll be here with you, and I fear that no one will come with flowers for us, or remember who we are."

He sat gloomily, watching the rising sun burnish the desert. Then he rose.

"At least you're near home," he said. "Most of your life was spent here in this blessed place. For me it will be different, this change so late in my years."

He breakfasted and then called Maria and the capitán to his study. There was something palpably lovely about his daughter as she entered, and he was faintly surprised. She was fresh, even after the exhausting day.

"We are moving to Mexico where we belong," Ignacio announced abruptly.

"You'll sell the United States portion then?" asked the capitán.

The patrón paused. "No. To sell it I must have title in their records. I won't record the grant. Not to my dying day. And another thing. When we leave, the flag of Mexico will continue to fly here. We won't take it down when we go."

"Will it be Tres Arroyos, Papa?"

"Yes. We'll start enlarging our casa there at once. Capitán, you will arrange an orderly move. The possessions, the cattle, all of it. The grass will come fast now, and they can be grazed southward with no loss. I see that some wagons have been salvaged. More can be repaired. Some of our vaqueros can be sent ahead to prepare down there. I leave it all to you, my Capitán."

He paused, and his bearing suddenly became hard.

"Capitán, as soon as you have the moving organized, you will attend to some other business without fail. You, Gomez, and Juanito will attend to it, and you won't return until it's done."

"I understand perfectly," the capitán replied.

"If you want, take more pistoleros with you. Whatever you need. The important thing is to complete your mission!"

"It will be dangerous for you, Pedro," Maria said unhappily.

Don Ignacio realized from her tone of voice what had transformed his daughter. He glanced at them both. Well, he thought, they would seek his permission in good time. It was desirable. That was the way things happened in life, the bad and the good. In time there would be an heir . . . a grandson. Tres Arroyos would see a wedding!

"Be careful, my Capitán," he said edgily. "Be very careful. We have had too much grief already."

"It will be a good new life for us all, Papa." Maria beamed after the capitán had left them.

CHAPTER 14

Nathaniel stuck to the firm wagon road until the storm had passed. The last light faded, but as long as he walked the mule team he was able to keep them in the starlit ruts. At a point about twenty miles north of the hacienda, where the land looked dry, he turned west toward the black bulk of Baboquivari.

He heard running water and halted the mules just short of a flooded arroyo, fed by mountain rains. He turned north into rockier country and drove until he smacked into a low ledge he had missed in the blackness. The jolt knocked him into the traces.

It was time to quit. He would have to wait for daylight to assess the damage. He turned the mules loose, except for General Sherman. They wouldn't drift far. He pulled his bedroll and food from the boot, and ate a cold meal, not daring to have a fire. Then he unrolled the blanket in the wagon bed, but it was hard and he was a long time falling asleep.

He awakened to one of the most astonishing sunrises he had ever seen. There were towers of cumulus rising majestically across the heavens, and the sun's first rays caught their catapulting walls and turned them salmon, gold, and yellow against a green heaven. There'd be more storms soon.

He felt rested. It was over. He didn't know how effective the blast was, but he knew the blast had occurred and he had heard the roar of water. At the least, he figured, the water washed away the corrals and scattered stock. That was comforting. It meant he had some lead time.

As soon as Jon was better they would leave the country. He didn't want to, but the gulf that separated him from Patience gave him no other option. There was still danger, but they were safer than they had been. Olivera would be too busy bailing out to give chase. If trouble did come, the monk and the Papago boys could help move Jon on a litter.

Nathaniel frowned. He remembered the report of the black horse near the cave and Night Hawk's certitude that the killer hombre was up there. There could be no safety, not even in Brother Pierre's canyon, while that murderer roamed the mountains.

He rose quickly. The Papago youths and the friar were little enough protection against a manhunter like that. He saw the wagon wheel then, and stared bitterly. The iron tire was half off and several spokes had cracked. It could be repaired, but he would have to bring tools and some new spokes and spend a day or two at it. The wagon would have to stay. That wasn't so bad, he thought. It was safer here than most places.

He walked up a rise and spotted the mules in a draw. He decided to abandon them for the time being: they would find ample water and forage here this time of year. Still, they might drift and he might never see them again.

General Sherman had grazed a perfect circle around the mesquite to which he was tied, but his orbits had gradually shrunk as the rope wound itself around the tree. Now he stood quietly under its low limbs. Nathaniel released and watered him and then threw his packsaddle on him. He emptied the boot and loaded his canteen, food, bedroll, and ammunition on the beast. Then he stored as much harness as he could in the boot, safe from the fierce sun, and departed toward the sacred peak afoot.

His destiny was the cave. He would have to be extremely careful to avoid a fight with that killer. But at least he could determine if anyone was there, whether there was danger, and what could be done. If he went home first, Patience would make a scene and not want him to leave again, and they would all sit there like ducks while that puma of a man roamed above.

The thought of his trouble with Patience roiled him. She wanted an illusory safety, he thought irritably. Together in the canyon while the lions stalked. Why wouldn't she understand that they were safe because he had reached out to the enemy and put a price on Olivera's deeds? He couldn't explain it. She would listen and not understand.

Maybe she was right about Concord, he thought gloomily. He just couldn't figure out the right and wrong of it. He tugged General Sherman's halter shank irritably and started up the long ridge to the shoulders of Baboquivari.

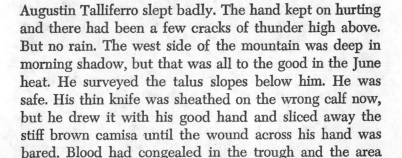

Augustin Talliferro slept badly. The hand kept on hurting and there had been a few cracks of thunder high above. But no rain. The west side of the mountain was deep in morning shadow, but that was all to the good in the June heat. He surveyed the talus slopes below him. He was safe. His thin knife was sheathed on the wrong calf now, but he drew it with his good hand and sliced away the stiff brown camisa until the wound across his hand was bared. Blood had congealed in the trough and the area was swollen. He couldn't even move his thumb normally. Carefully, he wrapped the hand in clean cotton from the barrel and knotted it with strips of cloth.

Still, he was functioning better than he supposed he could. The next step was the holster, which now hung from the wrong side. It consisted of a heavy leather back piece and a conical cup of leather laced to the back piece. The conical piece was cut off at the bottom so that the muzzle of the pistol could project through. He studied the holster leisurely, and realized he could reverse it to left-hand use simply by lacing the conical piece to the reverse side of the back piece.

He worked slowly with his good hand while he pinioned the leather in his bad one. He was in no hurry, and while he laced it together he congratulated himself on his intelligence and dexterity. He finished in the middle of the afternoon and joyously anchored the holster on his left hip and dropped the pistol into it. He stood at the top of the talus for hours, ecstatically whipping out the pistol with his left hand.

Then he turned to the carbine and found it gave him much more trouble. The butt was against the wrong shoulder and the wrong fingers were on the trigger. He didn't like it. Worse, it was clumsy to load with one hand. He practiced, but it was a miserable task.

He gave up on the carbine and turned to his knife after moving the sheath to his left calf. It felt good. That left only the Derringer in the pouch sewn to his right boot. There was nothing he could do about that. But he could still draw it if he had to.

At close quarters, he reflected, he was as deadly as ever. Only at a distance, where the carbine was involved, had he suffered any weakness from the wound. He would, therefore, use suitable tactics and work close. It pleased him that he thought through such details, unlike the mass of men. When the hand was better he would finish his work here and retire to Majorca in luxury.

He loafed in the cave for two days, leaving only to water the black mare. The pain persisted but he had become inured to it and had even forced himself to use the wounded hand a bit, just to discover the limits of his endurance. He congratulated himself on his will power. The man who stretched his talents beyond endurance was the man who triumphed.

By noon of San Juan's Day the sky was clouded over and sudden cool breezes leaped up from nowhere. By midafternoon Talliferro could hear a continuous bass-drum boom far to the east, beyond the peak. An hour later the storm had become a snare-drum rattle high above him and the light flickered violently outside the cave. Gusts of icy air eddied into his refuge.

Rain came suddenly, a deluge from above, and lightning struck fearsomely all about. A terrible luminous ball of light rolled down the talus. He noticed a small rivulet running under the barrels, formed by a sheet of water cascading down from above. He wrestled the barrels to higher ground and watched the water collect in the pool at the rear. The rivulet grew into a two-foot-wide flood and the pool began to march up the floor toward him. Talliferro watched with mounting dread.

The water deluged in, dropping in a single mass off the cliff. Within seconds a foot-high current poured into the cave. Talliferro raced to drag the barrels out into the storm, ignoring the screaming pain in his arm as he wrestled the barrels through the icy water. He was soaked and the cave was chest-deep. A bolt seared down and knocked him flat into the talus, and the crack wounded his ears. A second bolt struck just to the left, making unthinkable noise, and Talliferro screamed.

"Mother of God!" he cried as the thunder rattled his

muscles and spasmed his chest. Mother of God. He
blessed himself as a white sheet exploded a piñon pine on
a ledge just above, sending smoking splinters down on
him. He was terrified to be alive.

But he lived. The storm eddied off, and the night settled over Augustin Talliferro, who sat before the flooded
cave, drenched, cold, and addled. He couldn't think. Explosions boomed in his skull. Violent light battered his
eyes. So he sat in a wet stupor until the gray dawn, and
continued to sit while the sun rose and roasted him.

The glare of the day made Nathaniel squint. His head
ached from the unaccustomed tension of the muscles
around his eyes. Through those slits he studied everything ahead, alert for the glint of a rifle barrel in the sun.

He reached the base of the talus slope and paused in
the shadow of a juniper, studying the scene. He thought
he saw a man sitting in the talus near the great blue rock.
He couldn't be sure. He stared until the scene was fo-
cused better. There was a man, all right, and some objects
around him, probably the barrels. Of course! The cave
was flooded! Nathaniel turned to study the lower slope
and spotted the black horse grazing in shadow. So the
man was there, and the horse was below.

He pondered what to do. He could get between the
man and the horse just by moving a hundred yards forward. But it wasn't in him to shoot at the man without
knowing who he was, and without provocation. He would
have to get closer.

He grabbed General Sherman's halter and moved out
from shadow, keeping the big mule between the man
above and himself. He angled upward to block the man's
flight.

Augustin Talliferro watched the approaching mule stupidly, and only slowly realized that a man was on the far side, offering no target at all. The mule was edging up to him, and the man behind had a glinting rifle. His lightning-scrambled brain began functioning at last. He realized he was cut off from the mare. He would have to retreat uphill, but an upward flight would give him every advantage.

And now he would give that hombre something to think about. He grabbed the carbine with his good hand, rested the barrel on rock, sighted the wrong eye while the wrong finger squeezed the trigger. But at last the barrel wavered down and the sights lined up. Nathaniel saw the movement and ducked just as a shot racketed down the long slope. It ticked his ear. When he touched the lobe he felt blood. It had been that close! Getting into a showdown with a gunman was something he hadn't planned on, and he was plain scared.

He peered from under the mule's neck and saw the man above darting north and upslope. The man had abandoned his rifle. Nathaniel coldly rested his carbine on the packsaddle and fired. He couldn't see where the bullet struck. He levered the gun, but the nervous mule ruined the second shot. The hombre above disappeared into a gulley and then appeared again. He was moving toward a ridge that rose out of the northwest and seemed to offer access to the peak itself.

The hombre scrambled up a long slope and then stood for a moment on the ridge, sky-lined. Then he began to climb with great agility straight uphill. Nathaniel didn't shoot; there never was an opportunity to catch that tiny fast-moving target. He plunged upward, and in a few minutes his breath came in hot gasps. He abandoned the slow mule.

There was a distinct trail along the ridge, perhaps the one the Papagoes used to reach the sacred peak. He watched the hombre round a hairpin curve above. Nathaniel decided he had a clear shot. He steadied his pumping body, and fired. The man whirled to face him, then bolted higher. There was a tiny pistol in his left hand; something white in the right.

The hombre came to a series of waist-high ledges and tumbled rock that slowed him down. He catapulted over the first and lay flat, out of Nathaniel's vision. Then he sprang to the next ledge and paused. He negotiated five more ledges that way, always leaping at irregular intervals, never giving Nathaniel a target. But Nathaniel closed the gap, and when the man jumped for a longer run Nathaniel saw that it was the pale one with the domed head—the one who had shot Jon.

He paused. Ought he, a Concord farmer, be tangling with a man as deadly as the hombre above? It was sheer folly. He was being set up for a certain ambush. Almost as if to punctuate the thought, the hombre bobbed up from a gray parapet, aimed, and fired a shot that struck only two feet from Nathaniel. The Yankee gaped upward and suddenly turned cautious. The hombre leaped over another ledge and out of sight.

A cold sweat broke over Nathaniel. Now it was his turn to face the ledges under the pistol of the man above. He could give up and probably die on the way down. If he backed away, he and his family would surely die. There was no safety for any of them until the man above was silenced.

He leaped over the first ledge and rolled tight against the next one. He sprang over the next and this time a bullet ripped into the volcanic rock exactly where he had been an instant before. Fear and anger raged in Nathaniel, and he jammed new cartridges into his depleted magazine. He would not quit the next time.

He tossed a rock into a bush just off the ridge, and a

shot ripped into its roots. At the same instant he rose up, leaped to the next ledge, fired from his waist, stormed over high boulders, and gained another hundred feet on the hombre. He saw a head bob above and he shot again and heard the bullet whine off a rock and whine off a second rock.

Then silence returned. His throat was hoarse. He crawled left and found a slit in the rock and jammed his carbine through it. Through the sights he saw a rocky slope of broken stone, the cap of the mountain, and some towering white clouds in the infinity beyond.

"There's no way down, *hombre*. It's the top. *Muerte, hombre!*"

The reply was a storm of dislodged rock, with some chunks the size of his head rattling down on him. He flattened himself against the wall as the rubble rolled over. A pistol shot whanged through the crack where his carbine had been. Nathaniel crawled sideways and bobbed up for the next run. But the hombre was standing erect, twenty yards higher, and Nathaniel found himself staring into the man's pistol. The shot whipped the hat off Nathaniel, and it floated out into space on a gust of wind. He flattened himself again and inched off the trail. Another shot followed him. The hombre knew where he was.

Nathaniel agonized. It was lie there and die in the next moment or run straight into the man above, into that deadly pistol. There wasn't much hope either way, but attack would at least give him a target. He visualized what he must do: leap, spring sideways, and plunge forward.

The hombre was there as Nathaniel leaped, coldly waiting for the kill. He fired, and the shot burned Nathaniel's ribs. The second and third shots followed as Nathaniel sprung right. Then the man bolted as Nathaniel lowered his carbine and blasted a wild shot uphill. The man zigged and zagged, and then leaped out upon the gray dome that capped the sacred mountain, a dome of gently sloping rock riven with great cracks that gathered water and hurtled it into space.

The crease along his ribs hurt like crazy but it wasn't bleeding much and he could see it had barely furrowed his flesh. He paused to gulp air. Then he cautiously eased up the last precipitous slope, fairly certain the hombre had run out onto the dome, and was forting up somewhere.

Talliferro discovered that the great seams cutting through the dome were ideal trenches. They contained stunted, lightning-blasted pines with gnarled roots that would allow a man to peer out and not be seen, or shoot from ideal cover. There were clear puddles caught in small bowls of naked rock, and he slaked his thirst at one.

He glided upslope toward the top of the dome, and from there quickly memorized the whole system of faults and seams so he could roll from trench to trench if he had to, and from pine to pine. Then he ran down to a large defile running off to the north, and settled down behind a pine with a mass of twisted roots. His sweat dried in the high, cool air. He pulled out his powder flask and reloaded. Except for the old hand injury, he was unmarked.

Nathaniel knew he'd be a dead man the instant he crawled out on that naked rock. If he expected to live, he'd have to outwit that deadly pistolero. He eased downslope to a safer spot and studied the terrain. There were no other routes to the dome. The ridge he was on dropped precipitously on both sides. But on the northern side of the mountain there was a tiny shelf, scarcely two feet wide, that angled sharply upward along a fault line. The shelf seemed to end at a vee-shaped crack that broke the dome rock. He couldn't tell for sure. The gusts of wind were so violent they would blow a walking man off that shelf. But a man might crawl on all fours out there, reasonably safe.

The trouble was, he would be carrying his carbine. It had no sling, only the thong on the saddle ring. It would be noisy clattering over rock and invite the *coup de grâce*. Even so, if he went slowly enough . . . It was his only hope.

He dropped to his hands and knees and noticed that his shirt hung low. Perhaps it would hold the carbine. He eased the short weapon down until the butt reached his belt. He was surprised at how large it actually was. The stock came to his breastbone, and the trigger was at his Adam's apple. But when he buttoned his neck button the weapon was secure.

He eased out, knowing his knees would be sore by the time he negotiated the distance. He refused to look off to the left into infinity, and stared doggedly at the stone inches ahead. The gusts whipped him but he felt stable. He came to a place where the shelf sloped out, and put his hands over and then eased his legs over, praying they wouldn't slide out into space. He panicked for a moment but got past the worst of it.

He took his time, covering a hundred yards in a half hour and another hundred in twenty minutes, worrying whether the hombre above would be there, or spot him. For all Nathaniel knew, the hombre could be halfway back down the mountain. There was no backing up, no crabbing back over that slanting place. When he reached the vee he realized it was a major drainage off the dome.

He felt sick. The cleft ran six feet or so below the shelf where he was crouched. That meant he had to slide headfirst to its bottom without dropping off into space on the left. At the bottom he had to squirm his body to the right, uphill, and bring his legs around without sliding off into space. And do it all quietly.

Ice gathered around his heart. He peered up the cleft and saw nothing. The view was blocked by a bend fifty feet up. About four feet in was a root of a pine, a root that offered a good handhold if he needed one. There was no more reason to wait. With clammy hands, he slid down on his belly, while the carbine scraped noisily. His hands inched down to the bottom of the vee and he began his agonizing right turn.

He got to the point where he had to draw his legs down and around, but as they lowered he felt them roll out into space, and then his body began sliding, slowly, sickeningly, down the cleft. He grabbed for the root and missed, but he dug his fingernails into rock and the sliding stopped just as his hips began to slide into space.

His fingers found a tiny quarter-inch ridge. He pressed his nails into it and pulled gently until he had gained an inch or two. He released one hand and stretched desperately for the root and didn't find it. But he found a small crack he could wedge his fingers into, and he pulled up six more inches, and reached the root, which he gripped gratefully until his shaking stopped.

He crawled silently up the cleft then, rounded the bend, and stared up at the hombre not ten feet away, grinning crookedly. His pistol pointed straight at Nathaniel's head.

CHAPTER 15

The black hole of the pistol eased down slightly until Nathaniel stared straight into it. A sinking desolation clutched him.

The carbine was useless, he thought bitterly. Or was it? He lowered his shoulders, swung right, brought his hand to his face as if in terror, found the trigger under his neck, and pulled.

The crash roared in his ears and the butt knocked the wind out of him. But the slug bored into Talliferro's left arm above the elbow, shattering nerve and bone and muscle. The blow spun the hombre left and his pistol shot splattered into rock seven feet from Nathaniel. Talliferro's useless fingers dropped the pistol; his arm turned red, and he staggered away, out of the seam in the rock, and west across the dome. Nathaniel, gasping for breath and crumpled with pain, watched him go.

Talliferro stumbled through a revolving universe. He was upside down; the sun was beneath him, and then beside him. His good arm was shattered and pumping blood out upon the gray rock. Two worthless hands. No trigger finger. No knife grip. He felt a coyote biting at his heels and he kicked the air savagely. He saw his parents staring sternly at him before their stone cottage at La Puebla. It was over. He reeled west down the sloping granite cap, stood at the brink, and stepped out into space.

The pain eased and Nathaniel stared cautiously around him. He saw a trail of blood glistening wet in the sun, and the hombre walking drunkenly away. Down the long gray slope. Down to the sky. And then over. Nathaniel shuddered. He stood cautiously, half expecting a trick. He eased down the rock, following the blood, but the pitch was too steep to trust his footing. So he crouched down on his sore knees and edged to the lip of the dome and peered down. Nothing. Only a slope, at times vertical, dropping down to somewhere near his cave. The altitude clawed at his nerves.

He sat down on the dome and stared. Here on top of this arrogant peak the horizons were at the bottom, and he was in the middle of the clouded sky. No wonder the Papagoes believed Elder Brother lived here. The air was crisp. He slumped down in the shade of a gnarled pine and let his weariness overwhelm him.

Far below, in the shade of a juniper at the foot of the talus slope, Night Hawk stood motionless while his obsidian eyes studied the sacred mountain. He had stood here for two hours, stock-still. It was something he had trained himself to do. Often men and animals had passed within a few feet of the shaman, unseeing. Now he stood close to the black mare and a mule with a packsaddle askew on its back.

The shaman heard muffled shots, faint in the high air, and he waited. Then he heard another shot coming from far above. Then a tiny man had appeared at the top of the mountain and had stepped out into space. The body had struck a steep ledge that had chuted it out into space again, and it spun down, rotating in air, and thudded into the talus nearby.

Night Hawk sprang silently to the crumpled body of

the Evil One, and the light grew brilliant around the old shaman and he had a vision of a circle of panting coyotes, all howling. The shaman sat crosslegged beside the mangled body and sang a great death prayer. And then, with a strength that would have astonished any onlooker, he lifted the Evil One over the packsaddle on the mule and lashed down the body. Then he walked up to the flooded cave and washed his hands carefully. He returned to the mule and began leading it down to Hapgood Canyon, with this gift to his people.

Capitán Castillo-Armas rode into the canyon with Juanito, Gomez, and four good pistoleros recruited from the hacienda's vaqueros. He wanted the action to be quick and decisive. It would be a hard thing, killing them all, but he had seen worse. Four times he had led Federales into the camps of bandidos, killing them all. Twice he had attacked the camps of revolutionaries, killing every one.

This time there would be no pause, no talk, no maneuvering for position. Just one hard blow. He organized his soldados into a skirmish line, with himself at the center. They trotted into the meadow, and then began an easy lope, pistols drawn, down upon the ruins of the casa. They swept past the corrals and shed but met no resistance. The capitán saw a cookfire and makeshift table at the shed, and he barked an order. The pistoleros wheeled back to the shed while Gomez raced to the stronghold and found the two Papago youths there.

The pistoleros gathered in an arc around the canvas flap, and six pistols were aimed, ready for an execution. Gomez herded the Indian boys up while the capitán waited calmly.

"Hapgood. Come out immediately. If you resist everyone inside dies. *Everyone.* Come out with your hands up."

There was a deep silence and the pistoleros squeezed hard on their pistols, primed to strike.

"Very well, then, Hapgood. The price of the Hacienda del Leon is death. *Muerte*. For all."

The canvas door parted, and six fingers on six triggers began the spasm that would kill the man who had ravaged the hacienda of the Oliveras. It would be over in a fraction of a second.

The brown cassock of a Franciscan emerged, and the face and body of a monk. A balding man with a strong jaw and penetrating brown eyes. One pistolero's finger was faster than his eye, and a sharp blast rended the silence. A bullet smashed into the monk's thigh. He staggered a moment, felt wet on his leg, and then searing pain. He steadied himself and addressed the capitán.

"Do you kill women, wounded boys, girls, and a religious?" he gasped.

"We want Hapgood. Send him out and the rest will live," snapped the capitán.

"He's not here. He hasn't been here for days," replied the graying monk.

"If you're lying, Brother, you'll regret it."

Shock flooded through Pierre's frame and his face whitened. Then he sagged slowly to the ground.

"Benito. Bind his wound immediately. If you've killed him, Benito, I will put a bullet through your skull."

The vaquero dropped from his horse in stark fear and found that the bullet had pierced cleanly through the muscle at the rear of the thigh. He sliced the sleeve from his own camisa and bound it tightly around the thigh until the bleeding slowed.

"Señora Hapgood. You will come out now. With the muchacho in front of you," the capitán barked. Again the pistols lowered on the canvas flap.

The thin voice of a woman speaking English came to them.

"Jonathan can't walk after you shot him in the chest," Patience said bitterly.

"Shot in the chest?" The capitán was puzzled.

"You know what I'm talking about!" Patience snapped. "Who else would shoot him but the Oliveras?"

"Come out and we'll see about the muchacho." He aimed his pistol.

"I won't!" she cried. "If you'd shoot a monk then you'd shoot me!"

"The monk will live," the capitán replied blandly. "I will count to three . . ."

"I won't!" she cried. "I'll kill whoever comes. You'll kill me and my children, murderers, but some of you will die!"

"Don't be absurd," the capitán said levelly. "We could punch holes in that adobe in minutes."

There was a long silence. Pierre gradually revived and began to listen. The capitán grew restless.

"I never expected anything better of you or the Oliveras," Patience cried, haunted. "Come in then! Do it! I'll shoot!"

"In the name of God and all the saints, leave her alone!" bellowed the monk, weakly. "May you roast in hell if you—"

"You whip and kill, like all the Spaniards—" Patience snapped furiously.

"Madame Hapgood, *silence!*" the monk roared with an authority that astonished them all.

The capitán, red with rage, subsided under the monk's raking glare.

"Very well, then," the capitán sighed. "You'll live, but Hapgood will die. Where is he?"

"Why must he die?" asked the monk softly.

"The dam. For flooding the hacienda. No man has ever struck at an Olivera that way and lived. The patrón has commanded it, and I will gladly do it."

Patience absorbed that with wonder. Flooded? A dam? Nathaniel still alive someplace?

"I see," said the monk slowly. "And by the same logic, whoever has destroyed this ranch of the Hapgoods ought to die as well, eh? Ah, justice!"

"You're on the wrong side, Brother," the capitán retorted narrowly. "And in very strange company for a Franciscan."

The monk closed his eyes while another wave of pain rolled down his leg.

"In any case, Hapgood must die before the Oliveras leave. It's a point of honor."

"You're leaving, then?" asked the monk.

"We're aliens here. Tres Arroyos, thirty miles south, is being readied for the Olivera family."

Someone was coming down the trail at the head of the canyon. A nod from the capitán sent two vaqueros wide to each flank. If it was Hapgood they would catch him in a murderous crossfire.

But it was an ancient Indian who appeared, leading a large mule burdened with something. The white-haired Papago was frail and erect, and his glittering eyes took in everything: the pistoleros, the capitán, the ashen-faced monk on the ground, with blood on him, and the Papago youths, squatting with terror on their faces, awaiting death.

The capitán realized the grotesque corpse was Talliferro. The monk saw it was not Hapgood, and a sigh of relief escaped him. The old one barked a command to the youths, and they arose timidly and stared at the Evil One, their enemy. One, who was baptised, made the sign of the cross.

In the shed, Patience was beside herself. "Brother, what is it? Is it Nathaniel? I can't see!" she whispered out to him.

"It's Night Hawk. And the body of the one who shot Jonathan. The one who murdered my sheep . . ." the monk said softly.

Jonathan heard it all from his bed in the hay, and his eyes misted. He eased the terrible grip he had on his father's pistol under the blanket, and lay back in the darkness. His chest hurt unendingly. He stared at his mother and she returned his gaze, smiled, and there was a bond between them.

Night Hawk walked straight to the capitán and stared up at the man in the saddle. Castillo-Armas had never felt so powerful a gaze. It was a palpable force emanating from a frail man of scarcely a hundred pounds. Not even the intimidating stare of his patrón measured against this black gaze. It forced him back in the saddle. It was unbearable.

Night Hawk turned to the youths and uttered a word. They lifted the limp body from the mule and carried it far off, to the edge of the meadow. The capitán saw a flashing knife and felt a wave of nausea rage through him. A pistolero turned livid, and another stared at the ground.

The capitán wondered how Talliferro had died. The body was pulverized. Surely the old Indian didn't kill him. It was Hapgood, almost certainly. Up there, somewhere, where the old one came from.

"Muchachos," he addressed his men. "The Norte Americano is up in the mountains somewhere. It was he who must have killed Talliferro. Let's go. We've a job to do, and we cannot return to the hacienda until we do it with honor."

"He who lives by the sword shall die by the sword," the friar said mildly.

The capitán's proud eyes filled with contempt. The
simpleton monk deserved his wound! He motioned
abruptly to his hombres, and they loped up the meadow,
and then clattered up the trail toward Baboquivari, and
the ring of iron horseshoes echoed down to the silent people below for a long time.

"Brother, it's time for you to get inside and onto the
soft hay," said Patience. "I'll help you up."

She pulled him up, and gently helped him in.

"The hospital." He smiled.

Night Hawk pulled the greasy shirt off the wound, and
signaled to Patience for water. He washed the injury
carefully. She thought it was strange that the wound had
bled so little. The ancient medicine man applied a curious
plaster, and then bound the leg tightly while the exhausted friar dozed.

The Franciscan had saved their lives, she thought hum-
bly. Were it not for his words, his bravery, his authority
. . . She paused before the cookfire, closed her eyes, and
silently gave thanks.

She prepared food almost in a trance. Her mind wasn't
there beside the steaming pots, but high above, wherever
Nathaniel was. She dreaded the news that would come
down the mountain soon. Dreaded it ever since he had
leaped onto the boot of the wagon and rattled down the
canyon.

But the strange thing was, she was beginning to feel
once again that her home was here. Her son was healing.
Everything had happened to her that possibly could, and
she had weathered it all. And now the Oliveras would
be leaving. And that strange, terrible man was dead.

The friar awoke, and it was apparently an event that
Night Hawk had waited for. The Indian beckoned Patience to the side of the monk and then began to speak at
length, with a quiet dignity.

"He says it's time for him to go to his people," the friar translated. "This is to be a time of celebration. He'll take the boys and the body and will go from hogan to hogan for all the people to see. There will be a great exorcism; the whole Papago people will celebrate. Then the sacred fire will turn the body to ash and the people will beat on drums to chase the evil spirit into the darkness forever.

"He wishes you and your family well. The spirit of Nathaniel Hapgood—whatever his fate—will hover over his people and befriend them, from this day's sunset to forever. And the people of the sacred peak will honor his spirit from this day's sunset to the last day, when the sun does not rise."

There was a long hush.

"Tell him Nathaniel and I are honored," said Patience, choosing her words. "We will be neighbors of the Papago people for as long as we live, and there will be hospitality here for them always. They will always be welcome at our home."

The shaman bowed slightly. He and the youths walked out to the meadow, wrapped the stiff body in a blanket, and carried it slowly down the canyon. A breeze followed them, rattling leaves. The crickets began to creak, and a blackbird in the cattails trilled a tentative note to its mate.

"*Que será será*," said the monk somberly. "I gather that you are planning to stay after all."

"Yes. This is where Nathaniel's heart is. And mine too, now. I realized today—for the first time—that my husband is up there somewhere in mortal danger to protect us. There because he loves us. When he left in the wagon I thought he was just trying to avenge us, you know, getting even with them in some blind, violent way."

She paused and the friar limped to the bench and sat beside her.

"I guess he spoke the language of vengeance, but that wasn't what he was trying to do," she continued. "We had news today. Something about flooding the hacienda. And blowing up a dam. And Ignacio Olivera leaving. *Leaving!* Whatever Nathaniel did, it's driving the Oliveras away so we can be safe. And whatever happened up on the mountain, the death of that terrible man wasn't for revenge, but to keep us safe!"

The monk's eyes glowed in the late sun.

"Most of it came to me when the capitán was threatening us," she said. "I didn't understand it in words, but the idea came. . . . Brother, it's very hard to be a woman sometimes. Especially here in the wilderness with its hardships. I took my children to Prescott and I loved it. I wore a dress that was flattering. We dined on linen. I enjoyed talking to gracious people. . . ."

She smiled sadly.

"But I'm here now. I've buried many dreams. I suppose that's part of being a wife and going wherever my husband goes. A woman learns to efface herself. . . ."

"But now you intend to stay—no matter what happens?"

"Yes. No matter what happens. I want to fulfill Nathaniel's dream for us. That's the strange thing! We efface ourselves and surrender our dreams and the next thing we know, our husbands' dreams are our own! And our joy is all the richer when they succeed because—they've become a part of us. It takes both of us to make them happen!"

"Marriage is a holy sacrament," said the friar.

She looked at him, mystified.

"It is larger and more joyous than self. When it comes alive, it is a foretaste of paradise," he said softly.

She smiled.

"Today, when I really understood that Nathaniel's risking everything for us, I also understood that men *must* struggle. More than a woman. More frustration, more disappointment. More jeopardy . . ."

"And more joy?" he asked softly.

"I don't know," she said. "We have joys that men can never know."

She stared up into the silent mountain, obscured by a black storm cloud over its shoulders, even while the peak was golden in the sun.

"I'm staying here. If he comes down from there alive. And also if he doesn't." She pressed her eyes closed in prayer.

The peak vanished behind a great mass of cumulus, and then appeared again, a golden shaft in a black sky.

CHAPTER 16

Nathaniel sprawled inertly on top of Baboquivari while his body and spirit mended. Then the afternoon sun vanished behind towering cumulus, and Nathaniel realized that he was lying atop a giant lightning rod. The blasted and scorched pines were mute testimony to his danger. He grabbed the carbine and began the descent, his rib wound stinging every step.

Spurred by the darkening sky, he sprang down the long grade rapidly. An hour later he reached the talus and began searching for his mule. He had the notion he might find Talliferro's body, but it was a vast country and if he never saw it he wouldn't have been surprised.

The mule had vanished but he spotted the black horse below. It would do if he could rig up some sort of emergency bridle. He veered toward the flooded cave hoping to find something useful in the barrels. A gray cloud lowered over him as he reached the barrels, and he found himself in an opaque white world. He found a roll of thong that would do.

He eased cautiously down the talus slope toward the horse. The fog was so thick he could only guess where it was. When he reached the bottom of the talus the cloud lifted a moment, and he saw the horse off to the left. And beyond the horse, a group of horsemen walking straight

toward him! The shock of it raced through him as the
cloud lowered again and cut off the view.

Had they seen him? He ran now. The black horse
meant his very life. The animal skittered sideways as he
loomed up on it in the mist.

"Ho, now, whoa," he said quietly, edging closer. There
were hoof sounds in the fog behind him. He edged toward the horse again, realizing it was a mare. She faced
him, ready to bolt. Eye contact. It was sometimes possible
to mesmerize a horse with it. He stared into her brown
eyes, talking softly, and eased the belt from his pants as
he inched closer. The muffled sound of horses beyond him
was alarming. The mare's ears rotated toward the noise.
She whinnied, and his heart sank. A horse out there whinnied back.

Gently he eased the belt over her neck until he had her.
She stood still. He unrolled the thong and slipped it into
her mouth, knotting it under her jaw. She fussed and
whinnied again. He threw the two ends over her withers,
and hoped they would do. He buckled the belt on her
neck and left it to hang on to. It would be better than
grabbing her mane. He was at a severe disadvantage
without a saddle, and the belt would help.

He jumped, then, clumsily, his carbine in one hand. As
he squirmed over her back she skittered sideways, and
then he was on. The dense cloud lifted again. A few yards
away were the horsemen. He glimpsed seven, and this
time they saw him for certain. He scarcely had time to
look, but the one, the capitán, he recognized instantly.

Nathaniel kicked the mare and she responded with a
lunge. He grabbed the belt and hung on as she plunged
forward. Then he swung his carbine back at the misty
group and fired into billowing clouds. Pistol shots reached
out at him but the mare had plunged fifteen yards from
where they had seen him. She was making noise in the

rock, and another shot—he visualized the cold, shrewd capitán shooting—whipped very close. He kicked the mare downslope, scarcely knowing what direction, hoping for more cloud cover.

He hadn't the faintest idea where he was going, but he was alive. If the cloud meant life, he thought, he'd better head upslope to stay in it. He'd have to take his consequences with lightning. He turned the mare and paused. It had become a deadly listening game. There was the sound of hoofs on his right and slightly below. Then the sound stopped and he realized they were waiting for him to move. He stood still. They fired several shots, but none came near. He didn't fire back, but used the moment to tie the ends of his thong together so he could drop his slender reins over the withers and shoot with both hands.

The mare chose to whinny again, and he kicked her savagely, grabbing the belt as she gathered her muscles and bolted up and over several ledges. Shots followed, and one buzzed ominously close. He stopped suddenly, wheeled his carbine to the rear, and fired into the white soup. Someone screamed, and pistol shots whipped back at him. He walked the mare quietly for a time, keeping out of clanging rock. He paused to listen now and then, but never stopped for more than a moment. There were no more shots.

The fog got thicker and he knew he was lost. He thought it was late in the afternoon, and he wished he could see the sun for a moment to get his bearings. If he could survive in this soup until dark, he'd have a chance. He had to avoid a confrontation. Those pistols could pour out death faster than his carbine.

Nathaniel was bitter. The pressure never ended. He had struck at them, and they had sent out mobs and armies. Now they would hunt him down on his own claimed land and haul his body back and drop it at Patience's feet—if they let her live.

Nathaniel's shot had ripped through the heart of Gomez, and he had lived just long enough to scream and then topple off his horse. They halted and gathered around him. The death had a sobering effect on the pistoleros, who suddenly wanted to return to their normal life below. But the capitán had a mission of honor, and he had no intention of failing. A rift in the cloud gave him a good idea of his position, but failed to reveal Hapgood. For an instant the capitán could see far upslope, to blue sky.

He paused. Long military training made him ask himself what the enemy would do in his circumstances. Hapgood, he decided, would stay high to take advantage of the cloud cover. So, then. His pistoleros would have to move still higher and intercept him. There was no knowing where Hapgood was, but if they moved fast enough and fanned out, they could form a dragnet moving downslope that would snare the man.

"Gomez was a good hombre," said the capitán sternly. "Lift him to his horse and tie him. It's a blessing he leaves no widow. Now we'll avenge his death. Find Hapgood and kill him. No quarter. We'll present him to his widow."

He led his remaining hombres straight upslope as fast as they could travel. For half an hour they never paused, but when the white clouds thinned and some blue appeared, the capitán called a halt.

He directed them to spread out until they were each a hundred yards from the next man. When they were all in position, they'd proceed downslope and trap Hapgood.

"Don't shoot each other," he cautioned. "Get close. Pause before you fire. Make sure it's Hapgood!"

The pistoleros sat restlessly.

"You'll need a signal," the capitán continued. "Tap the

butt of your revolver on the saddle horn, like so. See, the noise doesn't carry far. You'll identify each other in the fog that way. If I want you to gather around me, I'll fire three shots. Is that understood?"

The hombres spread out, frightened at the thought of being mistakenly shot, or suddenly killed by the Norte Americano. There were three to the capitán's right and two to the left, and each was suddenly alone in the whirling white universe.

Nathaniel walked the mare slowly upslope, ready to blast anything that loomed up in the haze. His mind raced, trying to sort out his strengths and weaknesses. He watched the mare's ears rotate and realized suddenly that she was his real weakness. She was too friendly; she knew every one of those Olivera horses, and they knew her, and they were greeting each other. One whinny and he'd be a dead man. He turned abruptly sideways, looking for a watercourse where there'd be some thickets in which to tie her. He worked slowly downward, his nerves taut, sweating in the clammy air. The mare's head rose; she sensed another horse and was about to whinny. Nathaniel jerked her head savagely and broke a thong. He eased off her back, mad at himself, and led her to a dark blur ahead where juniper loomed up. He tied her there with the remaining thong.

Then he ran swiftly up the watercourse, taking care not to rattle rock. He eased around some junipers until he found a dense pocket of them. There was good cover in them as long as the cloud remained. He waited, taut with anxiety, and then she whinnied again. A moment later she nickered—a sure sign that some friend was approaching.

A mounted man loomed out of the white fog scarcely twenty feet above Nathaniel. The hombre appeared to be looking across Nathaniel's thicket to the slope beyond, but there was nothing over there. The hombre began a steady tapping on the saddle horn with his pistol butt, and Nathaniel realized it was a signal. Far off in the opaque white came a muffled tapping in return, and Nathaniel knew he had a pistolero on each side.

The nearer man walked his horse quietly to a point just above Nathaniel, and paused again. Nathaniel swung his carbine up for a point-blank shot, and then decided not to. It would bring the others. Perhaps if he worked it right, he could bait a trap using the mare. He searched for a dead juniper limb and found a piece about two inches thick and a yard long. He had never clubbed a man in his life and he dreaded it. But he dreaded dying more. He studied the rock where he would step. The best route would take him right to the man's side. The horse turned to look, and Nathaniel froze.

He set down his carbine, counted three, and rose up swiftly. Two big steps, and *crack*. There was a sharp thud as the stick landed. The man toppled slowly off the horse and slammed into the ground. Nathaniel grabbed his carbine and stared at the bleeding face. It was not the capitán. He gathered the gelding, picked up the pistol, and began tapping steadily on the saddle horn. He was rewarded with a muffled tapping downslope on the other side of the watercourse.

His mare whinnied again, and this time two Olivera horses responded, one far off to the right, and one to the left and near. Nathaniel picked up the hombre's hat and jammed it down. It was too small, but it would have to do. He wheeled aboard the gelding just before the other rider materialized in the fog. He tapped quickly and the other rider tapped back, and then said something in Spanish.

"Si, si," whispered Nathaniel, as the man drew closer. The capitán! Another flood of fear raced through Nathaniel. He watched the capitán point downslope toward the noisy mare, and Nathaniel fell in behind. He eased the gelding closer to the capitán and reversed the pistol in his hand. The butt could tap heads as well as saddle horns. He primed himself. He was close enough now to be recognized if the capitán turned.

His heels touched the gelding again, this time bringing Nathaniel to striking distance. He raised his arm but just as he arced the gun downward the gelding pulled out. The pistol glanced off the capitán's head and stunned him. The capitán threw his arms up to protect his head, and his pistol flew into the fog.

"Hapgood!" he hissed.

Nathaniel rose up in the saddle and dove down upon the capitán's back, and the leap carried them off the capitán's horse and onto brutal rock. Terrible pain shot through Nathaniel's leg as they landed. The capitán was on top. He had the advantage of combat training, but Nathaniel was stronger after a lifetime of wrestling plows, and was goaded by a rage and fear greater than he had ever experienced. The capitán banged Nathaniel's head on the rock, drove a fist into his throat until Nathaniel choked, and then drove a knee into the groin.

In sheer pain, Nathaniel reflexively brought his knees up and kicked the capitán off him. The capitán rolled and then sprang to his feet before Nathaniel could collect himself. The capitán circled toward a fallen pistol, and Nathaniel lunged at him from his knees, caught the Capitán's boot across his cheek, but got the capitán's leg into his big hard hands and dragged him down.

The capitán chopped with his fists at the powerful arm pinioning his leg. Blows rained over Nathaniel's shoulders and biceps, and then the back of his neck and ears and head. He hung on stubbornly and then bit the capitán in the leg until the hombre screamed.

The capitán lunged for a hanging stirrup he saw just

beyond him, and the horse scampered sideways dragging the capitán with him. Nathaniel was raked over the raw rock and forced to let go of the capitán's leg as the horse danced away. The capitán reached the pistol and lifted it just as Nathaniel drove into him and sent him reeling back and the pistol flying.

The blow knocked the capitán beneath the horse, and the rear fetlock banged across the capitán's head, dazing him. That was all the time Nathaniel needed. He landed on the capitán and began pummeling him with his big farmer fists. Coldly, blow after blow. The capitán's lips split and his teeth banged loose. He bled at the nose and then around the eyes.

"*Alto!* Jesus, Maria, stop!" the capitán cried, and sank into a stupor. Slowly Nathaniel trammeled the wild fury inside himself and stared into the pulpy bleeding face below him.

"One false move and I'll kill you," he grated, panting.

"Enough. Dios," the capitán whispered, closing his swollen eyes against waves of pain.

Nathaniel straddled the man for minutes while the silent cloud whirled around them. The capitán's breathing eased a little and he stared darkly up at Nathaniel. They had beaten each other to pulp in two minutes.

Nathaniel warily eased off the capitán and picked up the nearest pistol, while the capitán lay inertly.

"Get up," Nathaniel snapped.

"Señor, I can't—"

"Get up or die."

Slowly the capitán raised himself to his hands and knees, and then staggered upright.

"What's your signal to the others?"

"Three shots," whispered the capitán.

"Three shots to do what?" Nathaniel demanded.

"To come to me."

"If you're lying, you're dead," Nathaniel hissed.

He fired three times, leveled the pistol on the capitán, and waited. Then he eased toward the gelding he had borrowed and slipped the carbine thong off the saddle horn so that he had a weapon in each hand.

When they heard muffled hoofs in the fog, Nathaniel stepped behind the capitán and jammed the pistol into his back.

"Tell them to come here. And remember I can understand a little of your lingo. Make it clear."

"*Aquí,*" the capitán yelled weakly. "*Por aquí.*"

The mare whinnied again, and Nathaniel grinned through cracked lips.

It was growing dark. There was thunder off somewhere and some rain in the clouds. Off at the limit of his vision Nathaniel saw the man he had clubbed rise to his knees, and then slowly stand up, holding his head.

"*Por aquí,*" said the capitán, and the dazed man staggered up, just as a mounted man loomed out of the gloom. The capitán didn't need to be told. The pistol in his back spoke to him. He ordered the mounted man off his horse and told him to drop his pistol and gunbelt. The two men stared at the capitán, saw Nathaniel's carbine lowered upon them, and obeyed.

"Tell them to lie on their stomachs," Nathaniel barked, and the capitán repeated the order. Reluctantly, until Nathaniel waved his carbine, they let themselves down and lay flat. When they saw the look on his face they covered their heads, expecting to die.

It began to drizzle, and the clouds lifted higher, giving him a view of some distance. A man on a rise far off saw them and rode over, and was disarmed. A hard crack of thunder rolled down the mountain.

"Any more?"

"Two. And one dead hombre, Gomez. All below. I can see them now. One is Juanito, the amigo of Gomez."

"We'll go to them. Lightning's coming. Don't even know where we are," Nathaniel grated. He was worried about being rushed by so many.

"Tell that one to get on his horse. I'll be watching with a mighty itchy finger. Tell the next one to truss him up with his reata and tie the knot good. If it's not a tight knot, he'll die."

The man swung up and the other man straitjacketed him and knotted the rope. Then Nathaniel compelled the third man to truss the second, and the capitán to tie up the third. Then they rode down to the twosome below, who stood silently beside the body of Gomez.

At the capitán's direction, Juanito dropped his pistol and threw down his carbine. The last armed man, a thin and mean young vaquero, had no intention of surrendering. He ignored the capitán's command and studied the gringo. He could take the man. He was fast with la pistola, and the gringo was obviously tired and had let his carbine sag. He eased his hand back, and heard the galloping hoofs of a horse in the distance. Nathaniel saw the man's crafty look and stealthy move too late to swing his carbine around. Then he heard whinnying and knew the mare had broken her thong and was racing to her friends here. The vaquero drove his hand down just as Nathaniel swung his carbine around. They fired simultaneously, just as both their horses turned to view the galloping mare. Both shots missed, and the mare plunged into the milling horses.

The vaquero whirled for another shot while Nathaniel swung his carbine around savagely and slammed the hombre broadside across the back. The hombre jolted forward and clawed for the saddle horn, while his pistol flew to the ground. Then the vaquero saw the carbine on him, a terrible look in Nathaniel's face, and knew he was about to die. But death didn't come.

The procession walked silently through the dark drizzle for an hour. Juanito led. His hands were not bound so he could rein his horse and lead the gelding carrying the body of Gomez. The trussed vaqueros followed, and then the capitán, and last, Nathaniel, who weaved wearily but never lowered the muzzle of his pistol. `

Nathaniel's mind churned furiously. He had a lot to say, even if it was futile to say it. He rode herd on himself as long as he could, and then addressed the capitán abruptly.

"Olivera wouldn't talk. I tried to be neighborly. Tried to get a boundary. Tried to negotiate. Tried to go to court. Couldn't even get where his boundary ran from him. All I got was your whip."

The capitán listened, saying nothing.

"I would have got my cows off the rincon. Next thing I knew you blew up my house and like to killed my wife and daughter. Made me a little mad! Maybe you'll be getting off our backs now and fix your dam."

"We're moving to Mexico," the capitán said wearily.

"Moving? Why don't you fix the dam?"

"Señor Hapgood. You don't understand Mexicans."

"No, reckon I don't," Nathaniel responded, and they lapsed into silence.

At the shed below they heard the clatter of hoofs long before they saw anyone descend toward them in the dusk. Patience walked out and stood quietly, head high. For days and hours she had been steeling herself for this terrible moment, and now she was as ready as she could be. She had prayed and had reconciled herself to the inevitable. So she stood erect, with only the whiteness of her hands betraying her torment. Brother Pierre limped out beside her.

They saw a Mexican youth first, leading a horse out of the gloom that was carrying a body. Patience watched the burdened animal with a heart that almost failed.

Then came a man with blood on his head, slumped in the saddle, and more men, curiously stiff. It was dark and she couldn't see much. Then she recognized the capitán, whose face was puffed and distorted. She saw Nathaniel behind them all, scraped, swollen, hollow-eyed—and alive! Her knees went weak with joy and wonder.

"*Mon Dieu!*" muttered the friar.

3 August 1874
Santa Margarita Ranch

The Hon. Jameson Canfield, Jr.
Prescott, Arizona Territory

Dear Major Canfield,
I am writing to thank you for sending the letter to Ignacio Olivera in our behalf, and to report that he has abandoned the Hacienda del Leon and moved to Mexico.

He took all his retainers with him, save one vaquero and his family, some people named Chavez. They preferred American citizenship. The Mexican flag no longer flies in Arizona Territory!

My husband succeeded, in ways almost miraculous to me, in a policy of retribution. After the Oliveras had destroyed our ranch and almost killed our son, he struck back, all alone, at their key water supply, a dam near the hacienda. And later he survived against Olivera's private army. How he managed only Providence knows, but I am reminded of your observation about men who have sand.

We are building new ranch headquarters down on the rincon, where we have a fine view of the peak. The pumas make ranching difficult in the mountains, but eventually we will root them out. Meanwhile the cattle prosper below, and we've found many strays, abandoned by the Oliveras.

If you should happen our way, the ranch is yours.

Respectfully,

Patience H. Hapgood